Acclaim for
My Father Is an Angry Storm Cloud:
Collected Stories

"These stories are coming for you. Some are deliberate shadows and others are monster babies, but either way you will agree that with this collection of Hawthorne-inflected tales Melissa Reddish claims a place as one of our most exciting American fabulists, alongside Kelly Link, Matt Bell, and Karen Russell."
- *Laura Ellen Scott, author of* Death Wishing *and* The Juliet

"*My Father Is an Angry Storm Cloud* takes aimless characters from the mundane world of suburbs and dead-end jobs and places them in situations where saviors can quickly become enemies, imaginary friends go on rampages and feral children will literally eat your house. Melissa Reddish is a brilliant storyteller who plays off our own fears of irrelevance and gives us something extraordinary to hold on to."
- *Jonathan Harper, author of* Daydreamers

"Reddish populates her stories with miniature men, bus-driving ghosts, and babies growing in gardens. But she also populates them with parents, children, and lovers, all struggling to find connection. *My Father is an Angry Storm Cloud* reminds us it's hardest to love the ones we hold closest."
- *Christy Crutchfield, author of* How to Catch a Coyote

MY FATHER IS AN ANGRY STORM CLOUD

COLLECTED STORIES

MELISSA REDDISH

TAILWINDS PRESS

Tailwinds Press
P.O. Box 2283, Radio City Station
New York, NY 10101-2283
www.tailwindspress.com

Published in the United States of America
ISBN: 978-0-9904546-4-9
1st ed. July 2015

CONTENTS

MY FATHER IS AN ANGRY STORM CLOUD

ROADKILL

When you feel the blur behind your eyes that will soon rip through your brain like wood splintering down a seam, you know it is time. Walk down the stairs, past the fake bowl of fruit on the kitchen table, out the front door and into your '91 Toyota Corolla. Turn the key and hear the metallic grind of the engine turning over, feel the first cool loosening of your blood vessels. Back out of the paved driveway and down the street you have driven since you were sixteen. Turn left out of the neighborhood, onto the road that leads to the forested area being cleared for development. Feel the anticipation on the back of your neck. When the first light gray shape bounces into your path, do not hit the accelerator—you do not want to give yourself away. Swerve only at the last second, the pitch of the wheel a certainty after so much practice. When at last you hear the crunch of bones into pavement and feel the small bump of your wheels, the last thin tendrils of pain disappear.

"Sweetheart, can you come here for a moment?" Casey's mother Nancy is standing in the kitchen. She is using her patient voice, the one that signals a request that is not really a request. "Could you rinse the crumbs out of the sink? Otherwise, they attract ants."

Casey walks into the doorway of the kitchen, her hands on her hips.

"The attitude is not necessary. It may seem trivial to you, but it won't seem that way when the ants swarm our entire kitchen. The ants send out a scout, you know, and as soon as he finds those little scraps of food you've so generously provided, we will have a full-scale infestation on our hands. Also, can you pull the shower curtain out when you're finished? If you leave it scrunched up like that, it will grow mildew."

"Okay." Casey has long since learned that it is pointless to argue, that any minor disagreement her mother will take as a personal challenge, one she will win by bringing up Casey's various faults: how she always leaves a smear of sauce on the lip of the jar, the way she refuses, absolutely refuses, to separate the laundry before heaving it into the machine, and her eye-rolling desire when she was six to grab all of the Kit-Kats from the other kids' Halloween candy. If Casey continues to argue, she will bring out the big guns: the tuition her mother paid for her degree in art history, the one that has led to such lucrative jobs as a stocker at Hollywood Video and her current employment at the Gap in the Centre at Salisbury, the one that has forced her to give up her apartment in Baltimore and move back home.

"Now, I'm going to the grocery store this afternoon, so please put anything you need on the shopping list."

"I can get what I need later."

"Nonsense. There's no need for both of us to make a trip and waste gas. Just put it on the list and I'll be happy to pick it up."

"Okay." Casey never realized how meaningless that word was until she moved back in with her parents.

"I'm making chicken divan tonight. Any objections?"

"Nope." Casey can hear the petulance in her voice and she hates it. She hates how she has slid back into the role of a sullen teenager, a dark figure that stalks the house and locks the door to her room for privacy. She recently found herself listening to an old Ani DiFranco CD and making gloomy parallels to her own life before she popped it out of the CD player and tossed it across the room. She has begun walking the length of the mall after her shift ends, wandering in and out of stores she has absolutely no interest in. She can remember when she was in eighth, ninth grade and believed Hot Topic was the height of goth fashion. She would wander into the Spencer's and become flushed at the sexy gag gifts, the dancing boobs and the dirty card games and the edible thongs, and then toward the back, the lava lamps and fuzzy blacklight posters alongside so many images of Hendrix that suggested a life she could only hazily imagine. Now she just finds it all tedious.

"And don't forget to wipe down the dishes in the top row of the dishwasher before you put them back in the cabinets. Sometimes the glasses collect water."

"Okay."

Each animal has a different feel when you run it over. The squirrels and chipmunks and damaged birds that can no longer fly barely register—a slight lift to the wheels and that is all. The possums and skunks are better. They are slow, laborious animals that rarely dart away. When you hit them, you can often hear the soft whomp of fur collapsing onto bone. You can feel the car pitch forward with the effort of clearing their bodies. Sometimes you troll the narrow roads down by the river: on one side, the old brick townhouses originally built for dock workers, and on the other, the subsidized housing. You do not make eye contact with the children walking the sidewalk or the thick women sitting on the bench, waiting for the bus. This area is overrun by stray cats, and you need barely turn onto the street before a black shape slinks by. The cats are always tougher—they are more cautious, more aware of their surroundings. You must drive slowly, achingly slowly, and watch the gathering of muscle on their limbs signaling flight. Always their bodies resist until the end.

Casey walks into Zia's, a low-slung brown building serving Pasta Steaks Seafood where the cute waiter works. He usually works the afternoon shifts, so she goes there for lunch whenever she can. After she is seated, she casts her head anxiously around and then, as soon as she sees him, she looks down at her menu as though trying to decide what to order.

"Haven't seen you for a while," he says. She discovered his name, Ken, after staring too long at his large, muscled shoulders and arms more appropriate for hoisting logs he cleared himself than gripping the ridiculously tiny pen and pad of paper.

"Been busy," Casey says in what she hopes is a careless manner. She finally looks up at his dangerously blue eyes, the smile on his face like a hook.

"Sure, sure," he says and taps the pad with his pen. "The usual? Personal pepperoni pizza and a glass of tea, no lemon?"

"Yes, please." She smiles even though her teeth are not as dazzlingly white as his, like a freaking toothpaste commercial. Last month, she tried using the Crest White-strips, but they only made the yellow stains on her teeth slightly more pronounced.

When her pizza arrives, she eats it with her book propped against the sweating glass. This time, it is Bukowski. Last week, it was Henry Miller and the week before, Baudelaire. Though he doesn't seem the literary type, Casey still chooses her reading selections carefully to cultivate an exciting and sexually adventurous persona. She knows a boy's deepest desire—a girl who can curse, drink scotch, and smoke cigars while remaining soft and papery thin underneath her gauzy pink dress.

Ken returns with her check, and on the back of the customer's copy is an address.

"Group of friends are throwing a party tonight. Feel free to stop by. If not, no big."

"Maybe I will," Casey says and slips the credit card into the black plastic sheath in a mysterious and seductive manner. Inside her chest, her heart trills.

After a long or particularly fruitful day, you drive back to your yellow rancher at the end of a cul-de-sac under the dark, starless sky. Your wheels and the underside of your car are covered in blood and viscera, so you unroll the hose coiled loosely on the side of the house and wash away the splatter, paying particular attention to your headlights and the grooves in your tires. You know you should feel a pitch of nausea watching the dark red clumps streak down the sidewalk, but all you feel is the tension in your fingers relaxing. You realize you have been clenching the steering wheel too tightly and you make a mental note to loosen your grip.

At night, you sometimes dream you are driving one of those monster trucks, a green and red behemoth named the Grave Digger, poised before a line of cars in a dirt arena. In your dream, you realize the cars are full of people, average people with average jobs—bankers and brokers and mailmen, all suddenly trapped in a rectangle of metal. They thump their palms ineffectually at the windshield, their mouths open in a soundless cry. You rev the motor once, twice, to get the audience pumped, to make the people in the cars think, perhaps, they have a chance, before you hit the gas and soar onto the top of the first car, the delicious crunch of the metal frame giving way to your tires, the windshield cracking and splintering and finally shattering, the person inside collapsing into a twisted heap of bones and meat. You drive over all of the cars, leaving a trail of rubble behind you, a ruined space of nothing but edges.

The party is in one of those old bungalows on Riverside often rented out to college students. This one is blue with white shutters, and it would be beautiful if not for the peeling paint and weed-choked lawn and bicycles stacked on the porch. Casey walks through the front door and into a living room filled with drunk college kids standing in groups or pairs and laughing. They are like an advertisement of young people having fun. In another small room, a ping-pong table has been set up with the net removed. Six red cups are clustered on either end. A young man with feathered hair slams the ping-pong ball far too hard, sending it careening over the edge while another young man with a large Polish nose effortlessly sinks it in one cup after another. A cluster of people hover around the table, watching or waiting their turn.

She squeezes through a throng of people into a kitchen with a mud-smeared linoleum floor and dishes overflowing the sink. A young girl holds her red plastic cup with both hands and stares up at a guy with a backwards baseball cap who is gesturing wildly and occasionally sloshing beer onto the floor. They look at Casey once when she enters and then immediately return to their conversation. The feeling of unbelonging is tremendous.

She continues on to the backyard where three guys are standing around a keg. One of them is Ken.

"Hey, girl from Zia's! You made it."

"Damn dude, you can't even remember her name? That's cold." A second guy turns to Casey and she can smell the alcohol on his breath. "If I slept with a girl like you, I'd sure as hell remember your name." Yes, but I would never sleep with you, Casey thinks to herself, taking in his short stature, his fohawk, his unlaced sneakers.

"I didn't sleep with her, asshole."

"Why not?" the third guy asks. He has dark curly hair and eyelashes so thick it seems difficult to imagine him blinking.

"Then you don't mind if I do. Name's Brian," Fohawk says.

"Casey."

"I apologize for these assholes. They don't know how to act around people," Ken says. He pauses, appraising her. "But it is nice to learn your name."

"It's okay," Casey says, "It's a boy's name anyway." She has no idea why she says this. All of the sudden attention has made her flushed, her head dizzy like it's full of helium.

"My brother's name is Kaelon. That sounds a bit like Caitlin."

"Your brother's name is faggot."

"Language, asshole. We have a lady present." Ken turns to Casey. "Would you like a beer?"

"Sure."

She watches him pump the keg, something she hasn't done since college. He hands her a red cup filled with mostly head.

"Sorry," he says, "it's almost tapped out."

She nods and presses the foam to her lips, trying to get a tiny sip of beer. When she does, she is not surprised that it is terrible.

"Want a tour of the house?"

Casey nods. Ken leads her through the dirty kitchen, punching the guy in the backwards baseball cap in the shoulder. He leads her through the beer pong room to the living room and up a narrow set of stairs. Casey has a vague notion that he should be pointing things out, telling her interesting anecdotes about each room or at least identifying them.

The tour ends in a small bedroom with posters of Biggie Smalls, Ludacris, and other rappers on the wall and an unmade twin-size bed shoved into a corner next to a window. Beside the bed is a bong and next to that, oddly enough, is a paperback copy of *Catcher in the Rye*.

"This is Brian's room," he says and once again, she is not surprised.

And then, without any preamble, he is upon her, his tongue snaking into her mouth, his hands gripping and tugging at her bra strap.

"What?" Casey says and then, "oh." They fall onto the unmade bed Casey hopes is not covered in bodily fluids. She tries to tell herself she is excited; ever since she saw him, she's imagined the dark red cavern of his mouth, his hands touching the soft flesh of her stomach. Of course, she didn't imagine him kneading her breasts quite so vigorously or rubbing himself against her leg. He pulls her dress over her head and yanks his own pants down, leaving them balled around his ankles. He then thrusts into her, and the sex is awful, just terrible, like a jackhammer or a butcher trying to tenderize a piece of meat. She holds onto the side of the bed with both hands until he is finished, which luckily doesn't take long.

Then, he is hiking up his pants and giving her a seedy smile. "Well," he says, zipping his fly, "back to the party."

He flings the door open and Casey scrambles to get her dress back on. She follows him outside where the other two guys are tapping a second keg. Fohawk leers at her and Eyelashes gives her a look of condescension or pity. For a moment she watches their exertions until Eyelashes walks over to her, his mouth set in a thin straight line.

"Is there anything I can get for you?" he asks in the voice of a man used to cleaning up other people's messes.

"No," she says. There is nothing she needs here. She turns and walks back through the house, out the front door, and into the cold night air. The noise of the party continues behind her. When she gets into her car, she can feel the first hot tremors of a migraine coming on. She starts the engine and heads north on Riverside, away from the party and her house, towards the tree-lined path of Pemberton Park.

The first time you hit an animal, it was an accident. You were seventeen and driving to a friend's house in Nanticoke. This was before the area had been cleared for townhouses and condos and was mostly thick wooded land punctuated with old colonial houses. It was dusk; red and purple light smeared across the sky like a bruise. You drove quickly and carelessly, certain that after a year, caution was no longer necessary. You were an old hat at this. One moment, you were driving the one-lane paved road, nothing but the beam of your headlights in front of you; the next, a large brown shape was there, wholly and irrevocably. You slammed on your brakes but already there was the sickening crunch of metal and then the world shifted. When you came to a stop, you were facing back the way you had come. In the glare of your lights, you could see the crumpled shape of a deer.

When you got out of your car, you checked your arms and legs and tentatively touched your cheeks, but everything appeared to be fine. One of your headlights was completely bashed in along with the metal around it. Otherwise, your car was untouched. Bits of plastic trailed to the body of the deer.

It took you several minutes to work up the nerve to approach the flung body. The deer was facing away from you, fur stuck out along the ridge of its back as though it was wearing hair gel. You couldn't see the head until you walked along the side, and then you noticed the long neck twisted toward the stomach. Already tiny bugs were climbing up the chin and into the crevices of its mouth and nose.

You nudged the body with your sneaker and it was like kicking a rug. The skin lifted and then sank immediately back into place. You kept expecting the deer to spring up, alive and pissed, or for someone to come along the road and scold you, but nobody came. The air was alive with the metallic hum of crickets, and the soft white hairs of your arms stood to attention. Finally, you returned to your car, the body of the deer diminishing behind you. In a moment, you would drive away and the body would remain, a ruined landscape, but for now, you simply stood next to your hood and felt the warmth of its exertions, the tightly coiled pressure released in a spray of blood and bone, and there was a certainty in the bump of gears below the rutted metal that you too were made of something more durable, something that would bend but not break. Once in the car, you started the engine, awake to the movement of animals in front of you.

BARLEY

The man inside the box is sleeping, nestled among a few wadded sheets of newsprint and a Pegasus figurine made with real fur. Rachel already has several fur-covered figurines, including a fox, a hound, and a rabbit. The rabbit is her favorite, ever since she saw the rabbits of *Watership Down* with their tiny-soft bodies and teeth gnashing and gnashing. Her mother probably shouldn't have shown her the movie when she was only seven: there was so much blood. Even so, it is the rabbit Rachel touches each night, the fur so soft, the body an empty hard shell.

The box is on her kitchen table, the cheapest thing with four legs Rachel could find at IKEA. She gently pokes the sleeping man. His body is wrapped around the Pegasus in a way that makes Rachel's bladder hurt like she has to pee. He wears a tweed jacket and trousers worn almost to threads. And, of course, he is only four inches tall. She pokes him again, and this time he shudders and rolls over.

"Jesus, God, what the fuck are you doing?"

"Language," Rachel says and is surprised to hear her mother's voice.

"Sorry, but Jesus, you nearly broke my ribs."

"And you almost broke my Pegasus." Rachel removes the figurine from the box and places it on the shelf with the others.

"Please don't tell me you paid money for that."

"As a matter of fact…" Rachel says and then doesn't complete the sentence. She contemplates sealing the man inside the box and sending him on his way. Instead, she looks out the window to the parking lot and sees the gutted Oldsmobile in the same spot as last week, two men lying on the asphalt with a single rusted toolbox between them. Across the street is the subsidized housing, where a gray-haired man walks his Pomeranian past an old black woman slumped on a bench. On the telephone wires above them, a pair of gray tennis shoes hang by their laces. Rachel isn't sure if they were abandoned by a group of kids or if they are a tattered signal: some invitation or warning. Once the sidewalk ends, the grass flows right to the river. At night, Rachel can see the coal mounds outside the oil refinery, and next to them, the shipbuilding yard where faceless men weld. She often watches the crackle-snap of light across the water and listens to the music from their radios. Once, she even heard Celine Dion. She imagined that she was on one of the pristine white cruise liners with a thousand windows, and after the conclusion of "My Heart Will Go On," the welders smashed a champagne bottle, and she was off, drifting into the bottomless night, each star winking the secret of the universe.

"Listen." The man climbs onto the table. "I don't mean to sound ungrateful—I appreciate you letting me out of the box. The cardboard was starting to chafe."

"What were you doing in there?"

"Travelling."

"To where?"

"Here, apparently." The man looks around, and Rachel tries to see the apartment through his eyes: the scuffed, bare walls, the mismatched furniture of a college student or serial killer, and, of course, the figurines. When shopping for a coffee table at Goodwill, her friend Samantha had picked up a cat figurine and held it in front of Rachel's face. *Isn't this thing so creepy?* And Rachel, touching first the plastic green eyes and then the snow-white fur, had felt a trill in her chest. *Yes.*

Rachel cups her palms together and after a moment's hesitation, the man climbs inside. He tells her his name is Barley, and she sets him on the coffee table.

"Got anything to eat?"

Rachel fills a small tumbler with water and Barley hoists himself up to the edge. His face makes small rings on the surface. Everything about him is miniature—his fingers gripping the glass, the very tiny laces on his very tiny shoes. She scoops a handful of Pringles onto the coffee table and watches as he navigates the edge, his face moving from side to side like an ear of corn. Rachel has the urge to gather more objects, just to see how he will interact with them.

"So, are you going to stay here?"

Barley looks surprised. "Well, if you're offering. But I'll need a place to sleep. I think your bra would make a sexy hammock."

Rachel shoves her pointer finger into Barley's stomach.

"Okay, okay! A shoebox filled with old socks, then. Nothing too fancy. But please, no more accosting me with fingers. I bruise."

For the first couple of days, Barley sits in the same spot and waits for Rachel to finish her shifts at Red Lobster. Some mornings she is nice and leaves him on the kitchen table with a sleeve of saltines. Other mornings, as she heads to yet another shift from hell (otherwise known as Endless Shrimp), she leaves Barley on the mantle with the figurines.

A week after his arrival, Rachel returns home to find Barley straddling the Pegasus. "I think they're starting to grow on me."

She begins leaving him on the tamped-down carpet, and he spends each day exploring the apartment. He climbs into the undiscovered nooks: the unwashed patch of linoleum behind the toilet, the dust-strewn expanse beneath her bed. He finds a chewed-up eraser, three soda tabs, a plastic vending machine egg, and a reindeer ornament made from wooden clothespins.

When Rachel comes home, she finds him amid his new pile of treasures. "Might be time to run the vacuum."

Rachel rarely cleans her apartment. Mostly she allows the dust to collect until the last Sunday of each month, when her eyelids tick and tell her it is time to move. Back home, her mother scrubbed every surface with Clorox Clean-Up, even wood, muttering catechisms to herself that Rachel would only catch portions of—"last end to all things" and "submit freely to the word." Whenever she sliced through a package of raw chicken, she would spray Clorox on the countertops, the sink, the floor, the lid of the trash can, and again in the sink after she washed her hands. She was certain germs lay coiled in the crevices, waiting. "You can't trust the first spray. You should always spray again, just to be sure. It only takes a tiny amount of salmonella to get through, and then you'll be sorry."

After one particularly grueling shift with too many women in knobby chenille blazers snapping their fingers and runny-nosed brats lobbing shrimp grenades and an unpleasant run-in with the sex offender cook who grabbed her wrist as she passed by the kitchen and said in a voice thick with phlegm *your eyes are green today*, Rachel returns home to find a message from her mother.

"Hello sweetheart. I know you are oh-so-busy, far too busy to answer the phone when your mother calls, but your father and I would like for you to come over for dinner Friday night. I hope you can clear a few moments in your schedule for us. Do you remember Holly Nelson? She was in your fifth grade dance recital. I was in line at the Super Wal-Mart yesterday and ran into her mother, and she told me that Holly has stopped returning her calls, so she checked Holly's bank account and found charges to a liquor store and some place called 'The Pleasure Dome' that is obviously a sex shop. It's only a matter of time before they find her dead in a ditch somewhere. Can you even imagine what her apartment looks like? Full of roaches and other nasty things, I bet. I'm so glad you decided to stay here where it's safe. I'll see you tomorrow at six o'clock."

Rachel climbs into her bed and looks up at the hairline fractures of her ceiling. If she doesn't do something about them soon, they will just get bigger. She makes a mental note to call her landlord but knows that she won't.

Barley walks to the edge of her bureau. "What's the trouble?"

"Bad day."

"Got any scotch? That always makes my day better."

Rachel shoves a pillow onto her face. She considers wrapping it tight around her face until she is stifled by cloth. "No scotch."

"You could tell me about your day. I could be your therapist." Barley clears his throat. "Ah, hmm. Yes, I see. Interesting. I believe you have control issues stemming from your unhappy childhood."

Rachel lifts the pillow from her face. "Obviously."

"That, and you need to get laid. I'm afraid I can't help you out there, though."

Rachel reaches over to feel the tiny knobs of fabric on his tweed jacket or the microscopic grooves of his pleated trousers—she isn't sure precisely what her fingers are seeking, but she knows she wants contact with him somehow. Without a word, he holds her still. He runs his feather-light hands over the whorls in her fingertips, presses her skin in and then out like a sigh. She can't remember the last man who was this tender with her. Most of them she meets at bars and, after two and a half drinks, leads back to her apartment. They love to grip a handful of fabric and pull. They love to watch themselves in the mirror beside her bed. Rachel knows they aren't looking at her because their faces are always the same: carefully taut, fervent. But Barley has touched more of her and with greater intensity than any of those men, and he has barely finished kneading her thumb.

After he finishes, Barley grins at her with the tiniest row of teeth Rachel has ever seen. "I have magic fingers."

"Oh hush," Rachel says and carries him into the living room to watch some TV.

At the end of each shift, Rachel reaches out to Barley and he kneads the skin of her knuckle or pinkie. One night, she places him on her calf, and his hands loosen muscles tensed from hours of ferrying trays. After that, she carries him to her bed where he attends to different areas of her body, touching the fine hairs on her wrist, climbing her tiny bicep, walking with bare feet across the spotted terrain of her back. He never says anything during these times—no double entendres or sexual puns. Afterwards, they return to the living room, and Barley suggests that maybe she would be more comfortable in her skivvies, and she pokes him very gently in the ribs, and the moment is over.

She knows it can never progress beyond this, that anything more would be unrealistic, impossible, and yet at night she dreams of his body stretching itself out, slowly, by inches, until it is the size of a man but soft like a pillow, a body she can fall into, over and over.

Her parents' house is two miles behind the mall, down a narrow street that cars fly down at fifty, sixty miles an hour. Barley squats in the cup holder sticky from accumulated spills. On Thursday, Rachel had called to say she was bringing a guest and her mother had sighed as though she had to rearrange the entire evening.

"I wish I had more notice."

Rachel shrugged, though she knew her mother couldn't see the gesture. "He doesn't eat much."

"He? Oh, your father isn't going to be happy about this."

Inside the fake wood paneling of the living room, everything is just as it was when Rachel lived there. Television trays are stacked against the wall. Above the trays are several collector plates featuring scenes from the Bible, and next to the television, a dime-store porcelain Madonna. The table her grandfather carved with a rasp, file, and several tiny knives has been pulled to the middle of the room. It is easily the most beautiful thing in the house, with its foldable leaves and precise lines running along the edge. Throughout Rachel's childhood, her mother usually kept it against the far wall draped with a yellow curtain to keep out dust and greasy fingerprints. The only time she took it out was for company, and the only company ever deemed worthy was Rachel's aunt Veronica who wore matching pantsuits and always brought a bottle of Pinot that she drank by herself.

Her mother thrusts a handful of forks and knives at Rachel. "Set the table, please." Her voice is heavy, exhausted, as though Rachel has been idly watching her mother work all day. The sleeves of her cardigan are pushed up, and the beading crinkles whenever she moves.

As Rachel places the silverware on the table, her mother watches from the doorway. "You cut your hair. It looks better long. More feminine."

Rachel sets Barley down on the table as well.

"No no no no no." Her mother scoops Barley into her palm and deposits him on the chair. "Dirty feet on your grandfather's table as though we were savages." She looks down and appears to notice Barley for the first time. "And what is that?"

"His name is Barley."

"How do you do, ma'am?" Barley bows in a perfect imitation of a gentleman, and Rachel is very proud.

"I see. Come help me with the plates."

When the mound of spaghetti is placed in the center of the table, Rachel's father finally opens the bedroom door. She can hear his footsteps down the hall—she knows exactly what they sound like. He walks into the living room and sits at the head of the table. In his right hand is a can of Natural Light in a Steelers cozy, the black foam worn to gray where his fingers clench. This is how Rachel imagines her father: slouched in his cracked leather armchair with a can of Natty Light. Once, when she was seven, he poured the can into his cereal and called it Beerios. Later, when she was twelve, he finally let her take a sip during a Steelers/Ravens game. She said it tasted like water and piss, and he hit her so hard she spun into the coffee table.

"Let us pray." Her mother folds her hands and everyone else does the same. "Rachel, why don't you lead us?"

"Heavenly Father. Bless us for thy gifts we are about to receive. Through Christ, our Lord. Amen."

"What's a little man doing at the table?"

"Name's Barley." Barley reaches out a hand towards Rachel's father. He ignores it.

"Would you like some bread, Henry?" Rachel's mother passes the basket. Rachel's father takes a roll and rips it open, his eyes on Barley.

Rachel twirls a couple strands of spaghetti and dangles them in front of Barley. He grabs a strand with both hands and tears into it like a plate of ribs. His hands stain red from the sauce.

"Why doesn't he use a fork and knife like a normal person?"

"He's too small, Henry."

"Doesn't seem natural."

"The Lord knows what He is doing, and if He wants to make a very tiny man, then it is not our place to question Him."

Rachel's father lowers his silverware and places his hands palm-down on the table. "I said, it ain't natural."

Rachel's mother leans in toward Rachel. "Why don't we move him to the kitchen? He can eat on the counter."

"No."

"Excuse me? I don't think I heard you."

Rachel crosses her arms. Her throat is tight and her eyes feel full but she is ready. "You heard me just fine."

"Who do you think you are?"

"We're your guests, mother. You need to treat us that way."

"You are acting like a child, and that is how I'm going to treat you." Rachel's mother grabs her by the arm. "Do you know where children go? Children go into the closet until they learn to behave."

Rachel feels a siren-scream welling up from deep inside her, a place that still fears a small, dark room.

Barley stands on the chair and clears his throat. It is a very small noise. "Did I ever tell you the story of how I wound up in the box?" He waits until all eyes are on him. "I was wandering through a cold Minnesota winter, through drifts of snow as tall as my head. It was nothing but white, and I didn't think I was going to make it. Then, I saw a little cottage bathed in light. It was gorgeous, I tell you, a goddamn beacon. Turns out an old woman named Rose lived there by herself. She took me in, fed me, gave me clothing from her dollhouse. She started calling me

Fred, after her dead husband. Problem was, the old broad got it into her head that I actually was this Fred fellow. She put on a blouse, tied her gray hair up in a bun, and sprayed some old lady perfume that smelled like rotting lilac. She even spread rose petals on the bed. I had a good idea what she expected, and I tell you what— I was pretty scared. While she was in the kitchen cooking up a roast chicken, I found a room full of boxes she was shipping out and crawled into one. It was pure agony leaving that roast chicken like that, but it had to be done."

Rachel's father chuckles and waves his hand. "Leave him there. He's fine."

Rachel and her mother sit. Her mother folds her hands together. "Would anyone like more bread?"

On the drive home, Rachel touches the soft mass of hair on Barley's head, runs her finger across the rough wool of his jacket. She wants to stretch him out, wrap her legs around his thigh until she is covered in his touch. Maybe then it would be enough, and she would not be back in her bedroom, eight or nine years old, hearing hard sounds coming from her parents' bedroom. Some nights that would be all. Other nights, her father's footsteps would sound down the hall. They were slow, precise, always headed in the same direction. Sometimes he would pause like he was just going to the bathroom. But then the creak-crick of his feet on the wood began again, and she knew. Rachel's arms and legs and the tip of her nose were tucked beneath the comforter. She imagined the comforter wrapping her in pillow-soft feathers that covered her tiny body in white. When the footsteps finally reached her room, she saw nothing but feathers, feathers, feathers.

One night, she noticed a tear in the flowered wallpaper and she dug a finger inside and the paper made a scream and tore from the wall and it was very good. She dug her finger in some more and tore off strips until she hit glue. Behind the wallpaper was white, dusty wall and the grit felt good pushed inside her fingernails. But when her mother discovered the mess in the morning, she grabbed Rachel's face, her nails digging into her cheeks. Rachel could see her crow's feet and the smudge of eyeliner applied so precisely that morning. But what she really remembered was her mother's eyes—all that blue boring down, as though Rachel's face was treacherous, full of some hidden danger just waiting to leak out.

Rachel begins to imagine how Barley would look as a full-grown man, though in her dreams he is not quite a man but a stretched-out version of himself, still easily picked up and tossed inside of a box. Would his hands be the same feather-soft nubs of skin, or would they be rough, calloused, a working man's hands? Would his face be creased with pockmarks from a childhood of acne? Somehow, she couldn't imagine the ordinariness of life scraping marks onto his features. She could only imagine a body ready to engulf her.

A week after dinner with her parents, she turns from the episode of *Top Chef* and asks Barley if there are others like him.

"Don't know. Never met anyone but myself."

"Then how do you know your condition can't be fixed?"

"My condition?" He looks up from the wide expanse of seat cushion.

"You know." Rachel gestures up and down. "Maybe you could take a growth hormone or something."

"Darling, what you call my condition I call my life."

"Sorry, sorry. Just a thought."

Later that week, Barley turns to find Rachel holding a tape measure. "Just to see if there has been any change," she says.

She calls her doctor, a woman with high cheekbones and perfectly tweezed eyebrows whom Rachel hates a little more with each visit. The receptionist asks what the appointment is for, and Rachel says that is between herself and the doctor. She knows they will be unhappy with the bait and switch, but treating Barley will certainly be unique, perhaps even groundbreaking. Who knows—the doctor might even be able to publish the results in a journal.

After she hangs up, Rachel sets the box with the Pegasus inside on her coffee table. She found a buyer through eBay and decided to send off the pieces of her collection, starting with the flying horse. When she looks at them now, they seem like silly, childish things. She grabs a roll of packing tape from her hall closet, and when she returns, she discovers Barley nestled in the same location as when she first found him. For a moment Rachel feels déjà vu.

"I thought it was time to be moving on," Barley says.

"I see."

"Don't take it personally, love. Just think it's time for something new. Fresh shores, new horizons and all that."

"I get it," Rachel says, even though she doesn't. Why now, she wants to ask. But there is a tightness in her throat that signals her own body's treachery. She nods, closes the lid, and seals the box shut before either of them has a chance to say anything. She grabs a knife from the kitchen.

"I'm going to poke some air holes. Watch out."

She brings the knife down on the box once and then again and again and again. She doesn't think of anything, just the working of her muscles. Bone and tendon loop from her shoulder to her hand, the joints acting as a fulcrum. She can almost hear her muscles twang on each upswing, feel the furious machinery of her body. But beyond this thought lies a peculiar empty white, and inside this white, something pulses: a viscous, seething thing. She turns her attention back to her hand bringing down the blade.

When she stops, the box is filled with tiny holes and accordioned strips where the cardboard tore.

"Still okay in there?"

There is no response. Either he's ignoring her, or. She pauses for a moment, the knife held still. It would only take a second to cut through the tape.

She grabs the box and tosses it into her passenger seat. At the post office, she waits in line with other impatient people performing their Saturday chores. The stooped, white-haired man before her takes a very long time to purchase a book of stamps and then place them, one by one, on the damp cluster of letters in his hands. She drums her fingers against the side of the box and then stops. When it is finally her turn, the woman behind the counter asks if there is anything breakable, flammable, or hazardous in the box. Rachel says there isn't.

She expects to feel guilt and panic clawing their way up her throat, but her head is a buzzing lightness. Someone will have to open the box eventually, but it won't be her, and it won't be here. Fresh shores, she thinks to herself, new horizons and all that.

She walks outside, and the sun cuts strips through a line of clouds that spread onto the cars in great smears of light. A siren rings and rings in the distance. It is coming towards her from every direction. Rachel knows it is the Doppler effect, but still her skin pitches and swells. The siren is an insistent panic-whine of need, and it is heading towards her. There is no getting in the car and no driving away. And yet, it is many streets away. There is still some time before it comes.

MY FATHER IS AN ANGRY STORM CLOUD

The sky is a long gray board tacked to the ceiling of the universe. There is a sound that is hushed under other, smaller sounds that are not. The branches of the tree outside the window are bowing. A leaf whips past, another. Places to be, places to be! They're all in such a hurry.

Teresa calls her ex-boyfriend and presses the phone to her face until it is slicked with grease.

"You promised never to take more than three rings to answer."

"Remember, I don't know how to communicate properly."

She pauses. "It's about to rain here."

"It's raining other places too. You're not special."

She considers this hard little nugget of wisdom opening and closing its tiny little fists in her lap. Its eyes are squeezed shut because it is new and it has been separated from its mother too soon. There is nothing much she can do for it.

The rain is sudden, tremendous; it sluices down her window in great wide sheets. Her apartment steams. She opens her window, and the rain falls inside and immediately pools on the floor. She wants to take a shower but she is afraid the building will be hit by lightning and it will travel through the water in the pipes directly to her. She shoves an entire plum in her mouth and chews and chews until she can spit out the seed. Juice dribbles onto her chin. She imagines she is an infant in a woven basket washing down the river. Who will save her before she pitches over the cliff? She sees carefully muscled arms, brown, reaching and hoisting the basket to shore. They are not the arms of her ex, so they have no body, no face. Just arms cradling the baby against a slate gray sky.

The rain has stopped and everything outside is dripping in a lascivious way. She opens her fridge and sees her father's head on a platter. She doesn't have any platters, so she isn't sure where it came from. There is no blood, just a clean cut at the neck. He still has the same military-style buzz.

"Don't leave the goddamned door open. You'll let in flies."

The door closes with a suction sound. She is tired of seeing her father. Yesterday she bit into an apple and found his teeth rattling inside. A couple days earlier, her sink was clogged with his beard hair. Last week she found a pair of his moccasin slippers leaning against her bureau. The leather was worn to a fine layer. She pitched them in the dumpster outside and came back to find them peeking from underneath her bed.

Earlier that day, there was a letter from her father in the mailbox. She opened it, but it was written in disappearing ink, and the words vanished before she could read them. She drew a hand turkey and stuck it in the mailbox down the street.

He left when she was ten. She doesn't like to think about it. He gave her an Indian burn when she refused to take out the garbage. His teeth were large and white. They gleamed. He liked to be the cause of goose bumps. He didn't like when her mother let her loose flesh sag into the wicker chair. He threatened to cut it off with a knife. There were 78 black squares in their living room rug. There were 318 flowers in the wallpaper in her room but only four curled black bugs on her windowsill. She pressed her finger into one of the bugs and it made a sound like crumpled paper.

When he left, her mother took out a book, *Clichés for Everyday Use*, and read the ones that seemed appropriate.

"Good riddance to bad rubbish."

"A penny saved is a penny earned."

"A chain is only as strong as its weakest link."

"All dressed up and nowhere to go."

She wants to punch her mother in the mouth. She wants to slice a thin red line down the length of her arm to see her own veins glittering. She knows she is made from broken pottery, worm guts, stars. Everything, herself included, is combustible.

She calls her ex again, but the voice that answers is her father's. It crackles through the line as though from a great distance.

"Did you take out the trash?"

Teresa traps the phone between her shoulder and ear. "I never take out the trash. My room is a sea of garbage and my bed is a boat I paddle through it."

"Why are you always such a goddamn smartass?"

Outside, the rain has started again. She can hear the patter on her window like the drumming of fingers. She looks out the window and sees that the raindrops are large hairy fingers trying to poke their way inside. In the sky, her father's face is a cumulonimbus cloud. His eyes are dark gray swirls of gathered storm. Lightning arcs from one arm to the other.

"Stop being so dramatic," she says.

The storm gets louder and the wind slams rain, leaves, small branches against her window. The glass rattles. She pulls a blanket up to her chin under the wrecked sound of thunder. Her father once told her thunder was the sound of God bowling. Her father is getting a strike.

"I don't want to talk to you. Go away," she says.

All at once, the rain stops. She can hear the sound of water pouring through the gutters into the sodden clods of grass. The water level rises, higher and higher, until it covers doorways, windows, small children and animals. Her tiny apartment is an ark. It detaches from the rest of the building and floats along the flooded landscape dotted with downed telephone poles, floating mailboxes. A small brown dog is sitting on a rocking chair and she scoops it inside her boat. She floats along the street that leads to her favorite Italian restaurant, the one with the basket of different flavored rolls. Once there, she will dock her boat and eat every single roll from the basket. She tosses her cell phone into the swirling brown water. A seagull circles, cries once, and then flies away, searching for land.

GIRL BAND

Me and Jaime and Becca and Chandelle decided one day to form a girl band because why the fuck not? We couldn't decide between punk rock and an 80s hair band so we combined the two with safety-pin dresses and Dee Snider's hair. It was going to be so totally out it was in. After that, we had to come up with a name. Becca suggested the Feminine Mystique but Jaime said that was too froofy and suggested Back Alley Abortions which Chandelle nixed because she's a closet Catholic. Finally we decided on Danielle Steel Gave Me Herpes because we liked to imagine that Danielle Steel was secretly a sexaholic and would drive down to seedy bars and bang assholes in leather jackets doggy-style against a dumpster filled with syringes. Our first show was at Becca's brother's frat party and Chandelle had to set up the amp right next to the keg which made us really fucking unpopular. After the show, Jaime did three shots of Jägermeister and left to go bang some dude with a fohawk. Another douchebag in a popped collar tried to chat up Chandelle but she poured her cup of Natty Boh right on his junk and he called her a stupid cunt and gripped his package like it was going to shrivel up and die. Altogether, it wasn't the kind of glamorous rock lifestyle we had been expecting. We had one more show at a crummy little dive bar with Bud Light and Miller on tap that Jaime got us into by banging the owner—a balding motherfucker with a Depeche Mode shirt stretched across his beer gut—but we barely made it through one song before the ignorant rednecks were throwing ashtrays and beer bottles at us. Becca got a cut over her right eye and smashed her bass over some yokel's head and that was the end of our set. We maybe would have tried to play another show, but a week later Jaime was late and we all knew what that meant. Chandelle said if it was the guy with the fohawk she was going to cut off Jaime's tits. Jaime spent almost twenty minutes in the WaWa bathroom while we took turns drinking a giant smoothie, and when we heard the ohshitohshitohshit, we knew what the outcome was. We told her to name the baby Yoko since it was totally killing our band, but Jaime really wasn't in the mood so we let it drop. After a couple of days Jaime told us she wasn't going to keep the kid so we went with her to the clinic, even Chandelle, and read the brochures to each other in really obnoxious voices. Some bitch in a tube top dress who looked like she just rolled out of the club kept giving us the stink eye so Becca told her to stop playing into the hegemonic male narrative and the dumb bitch couldn't figure out whether or not she was being insulted so she started texting instead. Finally, Jaime came out looking fucking wrecked so we took her to Sonic for some chili dogs. Jaime only ate about half of hers and we made a joke about her not having to eat for two anymore and she smiled a little, which meant she wasn't completely gone. We told her we could name the band Jaime's Unborn Fetus and she told us to shut the fuck up and there was no band anymore, and we realized she was right. We put away our safety-pin dresses, stopped using an entire can of hairspray each night, and returned to our jobs at Superfresh and the Gap. Sometimes, though, after we've rung up the millionth can of chicken noodle soup or pair of acid-washed jeans, we think about that kid, that little lump of cells that was almost a person. We wonder if it would have had a lazy eye or a lisp or been a real fucking rocker. We even have our own names that we don't tell the others—Janis or Tribeca or Siobhan or Rose. We picture tiny little hands and tiny little feet and all the tiny little things they would wear: hats and mittens and footie pajamas. We feel a stirring from someplace deep inside us and then get really angry and fist it down, way down deep where we can't feel it anymore, and then turn up the Dead Kennedys until everything else is obliterated.

PROTEST

The first time Jacob began protesting, he was just eight years old. Later, his mother Carol felt she should have documented that first day to put in a scrapbook—photographs, a lyrical quote, and a pressed flower next to My First Words or My First Day of School. My First Protest.

But Carol's immediate reaction was one of quiet horror. On the downstairs television, she could hear the newscasters reporting the details of the Columbine shooting on an endless loop. Carol had been trying to figure out how to explain the unexplainable, how to reassure her son about Monday's approach when she was already considering keeping him home for the day, the week, the month—hell, homeschooling was starting to seem like a viable option.

When she finally came downstairs, her son was sitting on the pale taupe couch with jelly-smeared Hot Wheels cars and old grocery lists shoved beneath the cushions. Instead of her son's brown hair, sun-bleached and feather-soft, she saw a paper bag with two Xs where the eyes should be. On the side he had colored a long trickle of red in magic marker.

Carol stared at her son for a moment, the desire to gather him in her arms momentarily subsumed by her disgust. When the paper bag turned, and those two unseeing Xs fixed their gaze on her, she swallowed her fear and asked her son how he was doing.

"I'm sad," he said, and the small, tender voice, the one that said I Am Yours, gathered her throat in its tight little fight and squeezed. She wrapped him in her arms, her stomach thrumming like a heartbeat. The paper bag crinkled against her chest.

"What is this, honey?" She began to remove the paper bag.

"No!" Jacob cried and pulled it down with both hands. "They don't care who died. They only care who killed them."

Carol looked to the screen. Images of the shooters stood in two separate boxes next to a layout of the school. A red line snaked the hallways, showing the path they had taken. She looked at Jacob still clutching the paper bag.

"Oh honey." Her heart crumpled at the thought of her son taking on such weight. She tried to explain how there was a reason for everything, even senseless tragedies, but as the faceless paper bag stared in her direction, her words sounded dull and insincere. She thought back to those black-and-white videos in health class, the children whose problems were easily solved by brushing, flossing, and eating vegetables. There hadn't been any PSAs on dealing with the ruinous fear generated by a 24-hour media-saturated, globalized culture. They both turned back to the news, which had looped back to the beginning.

On Monday, Jacob insisted on wearing the paper bag to school, and when Carol refused, he hid it in his backpack. The next day, Carol was called in for a confer-ence. The guidance counselor and Jacob's homeroom teacher spoke to her in soft voices as though she were autistic, asking her questions that were really accusations. Had she and her husband sat down and spoken with him about the tragedy? Had they helped him through the grieving process? Had he exhibited any other distressing behavior? Her husband had simply shrugged when she showed him the paper bag sitting on her son's nightstand next to the Stegosaurus lamp. He had been working longer and longer hours on his company's latest project—a visor that would automatically download a person's social networking and media pages and project them as a continuous feed in that person's line of sight. They had already solved the problem of transparency, he said, so people could still walk and talk and drive. The problem was finishing the prototype before some other company developed microchips that would directly implant the information into the limbic system to influence buying habits.

Of course, she was bound by the nondisclosure agreement her husband had forced her to sign, so there was no mentioning this to the guidance counselor and homeroom teacher now cocking their heads in dog-like sympathy. No, she said through gritted teeth, he had not exhibited any other distressing behavior. He was simply trying to express his grief and what, exactly, was wrong with that?

Would they have a problem if a bunch of kids came in wearing black armbands as well?

No, no, they were quick to clarify, they had no problem with protests, per se, but well, this was a bit different, wasn't it? Black armbands were one thing but a paper bag gunshot victim was really something else. Not exactly tasteful, wouldn't she agree?

I didn't think we were moderating the kids' taste, Carol said and learned forward. What about Bobby Henderson? He picks his nose and wipes the snot on his desk. That's not exactly tasteful, is it? Why not call his parents in for a conference?

The guidance counselor and homeroom teacher exchanged looks. Carol hated the homeroom teacher with her oh-so-patient voice and her precise little outfits like today's polka-dotted dress and half-cardigan. She was the type of woman who would purse her lips in sympathy for Carol's wrinkled khakis and drugstore sunglasses.

The guidance counselor explained that maybe if Jacob removed the Xs and the blood, they could come to some sort of agreement, but it was important that they all be on the same side here. Carol wanted to ask what side that was, but she knew she was turning into one of those unreasonable parents, like Sarin Greenhawk, who wanted to abolish competitive games like kickball and give the kids participation ribbons instead of grades. And yet, she could imagine the teacher at home, a glass of red wine in hand, telling her husband about this one student with the sad paper bag over his head. And the mother, always so frumpy and tired, even though she didn't even *work*. Who would let their child go out like that, she would ask in a voice pitched to near-hysteric sympathy. And the husband, a spectacled man in Oxfords, would reply, drug addicts, that's who.

Carol was not a drug addict, though some nights when her husband was late and Jacob was already in bed, she would sit in the living room recliner and watch the light fade on the far wall from yellow to orange to gray. Her eyes would grow fuzzy with dark but she wouldn't move. Anyone looking at her would say she was waiting for something—her husband's return, maybe, or the sound of Jacob's cry, but she wasn't. In that brief, unfocused space, she was smooth and flat as a stone, heavy with nothing, obliterated flesh. Once she heard the scrape of her husband's key or Jacob's small whimpering cry, she would piece together thought and fear and body, but until then, she remained in that cast-off space, gone.

She told Jacob about her conversation with the guidance counselor and his homeroom teacher over breakfast the next morning, and he nodded as though he had been expecting this the entire time.

"I've made a new bag." He pulled a second paper bag over the first one. The new bag had a pair of red lips and an X of black masking tape over them.

"Because nobody is talking about the right thing," he said by way of explanation, and Carol wondered when her little boy had become so old.

"Like what, sweetheart?"

"They say video games are bad. But I play video games and I'm not a bad person."

"Of course you aren't." She tried not to think of her own desperate search through her son's room for a copy of *Grand Theft Auto 2* earlier that week. Had anyone asked, she would have explained that one of Jacob's friends could have lent him the game. That wasn't her real fear, though. As she pawed through stacks of Batman and Robin underwear she had folded herself and then a closet full of Velcro shoes and Marvel trading cards, she had the bizarre notion that the game had somehow fallen out of the sky from a capricious deity bent on wresting her son too soon into permanent adulthood. Just the other day, she recalled Jacob as a toddler running full-tilt into the living room, naked, flailing his arms in a furious air guitar to Queen's "Don't Stop Me Now." When was the last time he had given himself fully to the mad, devouring moment?

"Maybe it's time to take a break," Carol said. "You don't have to keep this up."

The paper bag turned in her direction. Where his eyes should be, there was only endless brown. "Yes I do."

"But why?"

"Someone has to." A small spoonful of cereal disappeared behind the paper bag.

A couple weeks later, Jacob came into the kitchen covered in large steel chains, the paper bag still on his head. Carol had attended two more conferences in that time, the guidance counselor explaining the need for closure and a return to normalcy, and the homeroom teacher explaining with clasped hands how the other kids snickered behind Jacob's back and tossed pencils at his head when she wasn't looking. Carol sat very still in the plastic chair and said that when Jacob was ready to take off the paper bag, he would.

When Carol reached over, she was amazed to find that the chains were heavy steel, not plastic as she had guessed. It hardly seemed possible for her son to stay upright, but he sat and ate his bowl of Fruit Loops without complaint.

"Our prejudice traps us," he said.

Carol tried her best to ignore the shift in diction and the possibility of a tumor pressing against his speech center. "Who are we prejudiced against?"

"Gay people."

Carol mentally reviewed the most recent news events, but couldn't think of anything specific. Finally, she asked, "Are you talking about Matthew Shepard? That was over a year ago."

"But I didn't know about it." The words stung Carol like an accusation, as though she had purposefully hidden this information from him.

From that point on, Jacob began travelling backwards. Each month, Jacob found a new tragedy he had missed and created a new means of protesting how it had faded from memory. For the Oklahoma City bombing, he screamed every time someone said the word bomb. For the Waco Siege, he wrapped his body in colored lights. For the Challenger Explosion, he wore a series of plastic rings around his arm. He moved further and further back in history until he had passed beyond his lifetime and then Carol's lifetime as well. Each item he piled on top of previous items until it became nearly impossible to find an area of uncovered skin. By the time he reached the Hindenburg, Carol stopped asking what his protests meant and simply watched the accumulation of items on her son's body, uncertain he was still underneath of it all.

Despite the onslaught of tragedies referenced on her son's body, Carol was unprepared when the planes crashed into the towers. She watched the dark figures pitch from the building and felt a stagger-step of panic as though the bodies were her own. She wrapped her arms around her stomach to feel herself grounded, held tight. A half hour of news coverage playing the same grainy footage again and again passed before Carol remembered that her son was still in school.

When she made it past the other mothers hurriedly pushing children into idling cars, she saw that her son had removed all of his protest gear. She nearly cried at the sight of his face, so pink and naked. He seemed so delicate, so unprotected, standing now in front of her, too easily ferreted by the wind whipping through the crowd of people.

Throughout the drive home, Carol glanced in the rearview mirror but stopped before saying anything. She watched the shifting panorama of emotion on her son's face as he stared out the window. How long had it been since she had seen worry or fear or desire etched in such direct lines? How long had she inferred what he was feeling through the sweep of his hands, the tone of his voice?

Back home, Jacob walked up to his room and closed the door. Carol listened to the same breathless recaps, hoping to hear a cluster of words she could offer her son, some way to make sense of the senseless. When she heard his footsteps on the stairs, she turned, determined to say whatever popped into her head. Jacob was wrapped head to toe in Ace bandages.

Carol resisted the urge to scream. Now look, she wanted to say, you cannot protest something that is currently happening. It doesn't work that way. But maybe, she realized, he wasn't protesting at all, maybe this was how he processed things now. It was almost comforting, being wrapped up like that. Carol too wished she could curl up into a blanket and have her mother rub her back, but of course, her mother had died of ovarian cancer when Jacob was five. By the time she had been diagnosed, the tumor had spread beyond her ovaries. She had refused treatment, explaining that the Lord took care of his own. In her final days, Carol made the trip to upstate New York and sat in the stifling dark room while endless episodes of *The Price is Right* played on the small black and white Zenith. She tried not to look at her mother's face or touch the rice-paper skin of her hand or follow the tube to the morphine drip beside the bed. On the nightstand were an unopened sleeve of saltines and the copy of the Bible Carol had often been forced to read passages of while her mother pan-fried pork chops for dinner. While her mother slept, Carol opened to the bookmarked page. 2 Corinthians 12. She murmured the words to herself. "That is why, for Christ's sake, I delight in weaknesses, in insults, in hardships, in persecutions, in difficulties. For when I am weak, then I am strong." She set the book on the nightstand. Hogwash.

The flags had gone up around the neighborhood with clever catchphrases like "United We Stand" and "These Colors Don't Run." Carol loaded her son in the backseat to drive them to the store. Despite the fact that her husband would probably be late for dinner, again, she was going to make roast chicken. As they drove down Rt. 13, the Outten Brothers sign flashed "Our Sympathy to the Families of 9/11" and then, immediately afterward, "Half-price Sealy Mattresses. Come in Today!" Carol glanced in the rearview mirror at her mummy son and felt for a moment as though she were not driving but floating, her car a steel boat slicing through the universe. As she pulled into the Giant parking lot, she wasn't even surprised at the number of cars at 8:30am on a Sunday.

She pushed a cart with one hand, and with the other she held the bandage-wrapped hand of her son. Several times she had to stop to correct the motion of the cart, until finally, she let go of Jacob's hand. "Stay close," she said. She led them through produce and dairy, trying to ignore the stares. She had gotten used to the attention of strangers when Jacob was a toddler and began to throw tantrums in the cereal aisle when she refused to buy both Boo Berries and Count Chocula, and then again when Jacob began wearing his protest gear. Everyone has an opinion on how to raise a child, even those who have no goddamn clue, she would tell herself when the soccer mom in track pants scowled at her or the two college kids in dirty flip-flops and thirty-dollar eyeliner whispered behind their hands.

She led them to the meat section, pausing in front of the display to choose a whole chicken. Three aisles down was the feminine products section, where she would buy condoms, lube, Monistat, and now, for the second time, a home pregnancy test. While focusing so closely on Jacob, she hadn't noticed missing her period until she was on her second pad-free month. She would have to bring Jacob with her, though she would much rather do this alone. Pulling down a pack of condoms or a tube of KY jelly while everyone else sought toothpaste or Tylenol made her feel obscene, like a greased-up body on display. How much worse with a kid in tow, especially one dressed like an old Universal Studios monster? But her husband had begun staying out later on Saturdays and Sundays too for the project, always the project, so she had no choice.

She chose a chicken, steeling herself for the final aisle. When she turned, Jacob was gone. Her arms grew heavy, and tiny ice crystals began to form in her chest. She flung her head left and right, angry at herself for not noticing and then at Jacob, who should know better.

"Oh you poor thing!" a woman's voice, high and pinched, called from the deli counter. Instinctively, Carol knew it was about Jacob. She dashed to the counter, leaving her cart behind.

A woman in matching floral print pants and blouse, her fingernails long and red, held Jacob by his arms. She plucked at the edge of a bandage with her fingernail, and Jacob tried to twist out of her grasp. "What is this, dear? Are you hurt? Have you been in an accident?" Half of the people watched the scene uncomfortably and the other half pretended not to notice, inching closer and closer to the deli counter.

"Sorry, yes," Carol said and grabbed Jacob. "He's mine. Thanks."

"Oh my, was he in a car accident? My husband was in one of those back in '98 and he had to wear a neck brace for a month."

"No, no accident. We should be going now."

"Should he be walking around like that?" The woman squatted until she was eye-level with Jacob. "Are you okay, sweetheart? If you're in trouble, you can tell me."

"Excuse me," Carol said, her face going hot, "that is none of your business."

"Oh I think it is entirely my business." The woman straightened and Carol could see the sweat-smeared eye-shadow, the furious curl of her hair like snakes coming for her, for her son. "Do you see what condition he's in? How can you let your little boy walk around like that and call yourself a mother? I should call the police right now."

Carol felt a tightness in her throat, a pinching behind the bridge of her nose. It was ludicrous, yet somehow she felt the weight of this woman's judgment as justified, inevitable. What kind of a mother was she, anyway, to let this continue for so long, to not find the words that would help Jacob shed these obscene accessories?

The woman hitched her breath as though she were about to scream, and Carol pulled Jacob down the first aisle she saw—Pet Food—abandoning her cart and speed-walking to keep her body from blossoming into panic. She tried not to imagine the woman giving chase behind her or the other customers stretching out hands to stop her, to wrest her from her son. When she reached the car, she buckled Jacob into the passenger seat and almost hit an old man wheeling a grocery cart in her attempt to get away.

Back home, she pulled Jacob into the kitchen and spun him around until two eye-slits faced her. "Why did you walk away in the grocery store? You know better than that."

Jacob shrugged and grabbed a box of Lucky Charms from the counter.

"No." Carol yanked the box from his hands. "We are not done talking."

Jacob pointed to his mouth and Carol noticed that the bandages covered it completely. How long had his mouth been covered? How was he even planning to eat his Lucky Charms? Though she couldn't see his expression, Carol could feel Jacob's smirk. A small compartment opened within her to reveal a twisted black mass that was hatred for her son.

"This is ridiculous!" Carol paced to the edge of the kitchen and back, working her hands. "You are too old for this." She looked at the outline of her bandaged son and waited for him to say something, anything. But he was silent, as though the bandages hid him from view, gave him an excuse not to engage with anyone, including her.

Carol suddenly felt another body ticking inside her, a drumbeat of insistence waiting to see what she would do.

"All right. Enough is enough." She grabbed the top layer of bandages and began to tug. They stuck fast to the contours of his body, and Jacob screamed as though she were ripping off a layer of skin. She ran over to the junk drawer and pulled out a pair of sewing shears that she had last used when Jacob was a baby and she had decided to sew all of his clothing. She had given up halfway through trying to piece together the pattern for a onesie.

Jacob bent over and clutched his legs. In a low voice, he murmured, No no no no no no no.

And then, all of her anger was spent. She dropped the sewing shears onto the floor and gathered her bandaged son in her lap just like she had when he was a baby. Of course, he wasn't a baby anymore—he was ten now, so close to being a teenager. She found the very edge of the bandages on his left hand and slowly began to unravel them. She worked her way down his arm. Underneath the bandages, there was nothing: no arm, just empty air. She kept going, unraveling the right arm, the chest, the legs. She finished with the head, expecting at least to find the paper bag with the hand-drawn Xs, but in the end, she was left with nothing but a dirty pile of dressings.

After a few moments of silence, she began to wrap the bandages around her own arms, to feel the sticky warmth of their accumulated sweat. She ran out before she finished her chest. Her son was much smaller than her, after all. She walked into his room and knotted a shirt to the end of the bandage, and then a pair of pants to the shirt, and so on until she was completely covered by his cast-off clothing. She placed a tiny sweater across her face, and as the world contracted to a point of dull green clarity, she understood. How much simpler it all was behind the mask, when her world was nothing more than the breathed-in sweat of her son. The truth of a body finally brought close.

When she removed the clothing, the air outside like pin-pricks down her throat, Jacob stood in front of her, ready, it seemed, for anything.

A HAUNTING

The haunting began on a Saturday, the day Holly once began with homemade bagels and now began with her daughter's leftover Froot Loops. At first, Holly assumed the smell was coming from outside, perhaps from the neighbor who burned leaves illegally in his front yard. But when she fully awoke, she realized, first, that the smell was much worse than burning foliage, and second, that it was coming from the house. She flung the covers back and ran downstairs, following the smell of not-leaves, not-wood, not-beef to the unmistakable red light of the oven. When she opened the oven door, Holly was greeted by a horror show of melted red plastic pooling in clumps like a tiny Jabba the Hut. It was Tina's plastic bucket and shovel—Holly could tell by the green handle stretching down, down, down toward the speckled dark floor.

Holly flipped the oven off, not yet wondering why it was on—any one of them could have turned it on by accident—but how the bucket had gotten in there. She assumed Tina was punishing the rogue toy after an imaginary infraction during playtime. Tina's bedroom was a constantly shifting landscape of alliances and feuds—Tony the Tyrannosaurus was married to Mrs. Bumblebee, but Bucket Head was constantly trying to steal her away to his sandcastle in the sky. Nuts the squirrel was a spy who was, by now, a double-quadruple agent. Holly suspected Nuts was based on Rick's brother Andy who always had some really expensive gadget each visit. Last time, it was a pen from NASA that wrote upside-down and also allegedly recorded conversations. Tina would whisper some complex, nonsensical sentences into the pen and then during dinner, Andy, who had an eidetic memory, would put the pen to his ear and recall the exact phrasing. Unfortunately, he also grabbed his junk at least once a visit and yelled, "That's a lot of nuts!"

"What time is it?" Rick walked down the stairs, rubbing his glasses in a creaking of plastic.

"Quarter of six."

"Are you cooking something?"

"Seriously? That's what my food smells like?"

Rick opened his eyes, then narrowed them. He opened the oven door, stared at the melted plastic for a few moments, and then closed the door. "Tina?"

Holly shrugged. They both knew it wasn't Tyler. While Tyler was interested in the inner workings of things, dismantling old modems and cell phones and a transistor radio he found at a garage sale, he understood well enough how plastic reacted to heat.

Upstairs, a burbling swell of nonsense grew louder and became the thump-thump-thump of Tina's feet down the stairs. Tina still had on her Dora footie pajamas, but she had pulled a sequined tutu on over top.

"Mr. Eggy Toast?"

Mr. Eggy Toast was a recent invention of Tina's involving a slice of toast underneath two poached eggs made from the microwavable egg cooker and a smear of strawberry jam in the shape of a grin. Holly thought he looked like a homicidal clown with his rheumy eyes and slimy red mouth, but Tina loved him. She would often lecture Mr. Eggy Toast on proper table etiquette and spear him through the eye with a butter knife when he got out of line.

"Did you do this?" Rick yanked the oven door, and it fell open in a clatter.

"Bucket Face!" Tina screamed and ran towards the oven. Holly managed to grab her by the tutu before she passed.

"Jesus, Rick," Holly said, trying to squeeze the hiccupping cries out of Tina, "Did you want to decapitate her dolls as well? Maybe leave them in her bed?"

"Actions have consequences. She has to learn."

"At least wait until the oven cools down. Or is a third-degree burn a consequence she should also learn?"

"Fine." Rick slammed the oven door closed. "You deal with it, then." He walked into the computer room, and Holly could hear the familiar ding of his laptop booting up. He would spend the next two hours scrolling through tech articles, and once Tyler came downstairs, they would have an extended conversation on unmanned drones or some other nonsense, leaving Holly to attend to Tina. Holly had tried telling Rick that splitting up the child duty like this wasn't fair—after all, Tyler was in eighth grade and could basically take care of himself—but Rick just shrugged and said that unless she wanted to learn how to rebuild a transistor radio from scratch, he didn't see what the problem was. Although taking care of Tina was undoubtedly more work, what Holly really hated was seeing Rick's mannerisms bloom onto Tyler—the way he tapped his watch before looking at the time, the way he squeezed his bottom lip when he was thinking—and see no such mirror in Tina. In fact, she spent most of her days certain that Tina was bored, her creativity unstimulated by Holly's pathetic attempts at playing, which were mostly re-enactments of her favorite episodes of *The Wonder Years*.

"Honey, I know this is hard, but when you put your toys in the oven, they will melt, and then you won't have them anymore."

"But, I, didn't, do, it," Tina said one word at a time through gasping sobs.

"Okay, honey, then who did?" A small, ugly part of Holly hoped it was actually Tyler, so Rick would be forced to confront him, and Holly could stand in the corner, arms crossed, shaking her head in silent disapproval of them both.

Tina stopped crying, her face holding in a big, puffy secret. She leaned close to Holly, preferring to whisper directly into people's eyes as though they really were windows to the soul. "A ghost."

"A ghost?" Holly felt momentarily stupid for believing a toddler might actually have information to give her.

"Yes, his name is Peepers and he's magic. He drives a bus and sometimes it goes into the sky and he finds rainbows and one time he brought me one and it was wet 'cause it was raining."

Holly thought about all the people they knew, and then she had it: this must be Frank Longman, their neighbor who drove the bus that both Tina and Tyler rode to school. He was a large man with a circle beard clearly meant to hide a double-chin. He always wore the same size-too-small yellow shirt that she and her husband said made him look like a marshmallow peep left too long in the microwave. She was a bit mortified to learn that Tina had not only heard them, but knew whom they were talking about. Holly tried to think back to her last encounter with Peepers—Frank—and remember if his wave had been warm and friendly, or an irritated flick of the wrist.

"Okay sweetheart. Maybe Peepers should apologize?"

"Oh no," Tina said, her face solemn, "He never does that." She leaned in close until Holly was afraid Tina's chapped lips were going to graze her eyeball. "He says that people have to accept what life hands them." She smiled. "What does that mean?"

The next event happened on a Tuesday morning when Rick and Tyler were already at work and school. Tina was home because she woke up with a "mean throat" and had spent half the morning doing her best Christian Bale impression. As soon as Holly agreed to let her stay home, her voice magically repaired itself. Days like these always made Holly a little anxious—an entire day to convince Tina that she, Holly, was an interesting person. Holly had even begun to watch old episodes of *X-Files* on the Netflix Instant Queue in hopes that she could steal more interesting plotlines for playtime.

When Holly walked into the kitchen to make peanut butter sandwiches for lunch, she discovered one side of the double-sided sink nearly overflowing with soapy water. Holly flipped the handle and pulled the plastic stopper. Instead of draining, the water just…stayed. Holly stared at the water gently lapping the side of the sink, a phenomenon she knew both Rick and Tyler would say was impossible, and then stuck her hand into the unpleasant hole of the garbage disposal. She knew it wouldn't turn on—the switch was right there—but still she felt a ticking in her throat. There was nothing in there: no mashed-up cereal, no chunks of chicken, no metal-gouged spoons. When she removed her hand, she heard a wet thwuck, and the water began to drain.

Either she was going crazy or Tina was deliberately trying to screw with her. This was not the first time she'd had to convince herself not to go head-to-head with a toddler who would never recognize defeat. She walked into the living room, where Tina was piling Holly's old mix-CDs from college into a tower that threatened to pitch off the coffee table.

"The sink appears to be filled with water. Know anything about that?"

Tina smushed two tiny fists against her mouth. "Peepers."

"Honey, I think it's time to stop with this Peepers business. It wasn't cute the first time. You could have burned the house down. Do you understand?"

"Mom, Peepers is real, I swear."

"Sweetheart, stop."

"He is! He comes in through the window and climbs into my bed and tells me secrets."

"Tina."

"And sometimes I get to stay on the bus when nobody else is and he takes me to our secret place."

Holly felt a squeezing in her chest similar to indigestion, except she hadn't eaten a meatball sub. It was her Mommy sense, the feeling that had told her in the grocery store last fall to grab Tina, toss the vacuum-sealed chicken breasts back in the display case, and leave, just leave, now. Later that day, there had been a carjacker caught in the parking lot.

She imagined the bus pulling up to school and Frank cranking the door handle and then, once all of the children were gone except for Tina, she imagined Frank, his jaundiced shirt bulging, cranking the door slowly closed.

"Tell me about this secret place."

"It's just for me and him, no grown-ups allowed."

"Isn't Peepers a grown-up?"

Tina sighed. "He's a ghost."

Holly sat on the carpet, eye-level with Tina. She had to take a different tack here—Tina would never give up a secret. It had taken her a solid week to find her sieve when Tony the Tyrannosaurus began using it to catch Mrs. Bumblebee and made Tina promise not to tell anyone.

"So, what do you do with Peepers?"

"We ride in his bus and sometimes we go underwater and see fishies and one time I saw a shark and his teeth were so big and Peepers said it was okay and that it wouldn't bite me so I rode the shark through the ocean and he was my friend."

"Does Peepers ever try to make you do something you don't want to do?"

Tina plucked at a clump of fibers on the carpet. Then she flicked a CD off of the tower she had created. The Bangles. "Can we listen to the Egypt song?"

"Maybe later. What does he force you to do?"

Tina shrugged.

"Can you point to it?" Holly realized she was supposed to have a doll, and then she was supposed to get Tina to point to an area that "Peepers" had touched. She ran upstairs and grabbed Mrs. Bumblebee from Tina's room. It probably wasn't the most anatomically representative toy, but it would have to do.

"Here, sweetheart, show me where Peepers, you know…on the doll." Holly found herself tongue-tied, holding a giant plush bee and wondering if she was blowing things out of proportion.

Tina grabbed Mrs. Bumblebee and began flying her around the room. "Buzz buzz buzz."

She was definitely blowing things out of proportion. Holly leaned back until she was lying on the carpet. She felt suddenly exhausted, and hungry, and then she remembered the sandwiches she had yet to make. Maybe she would feel better after eating. Calmer, more rational, able to accurately assess the situation. It was a common complaint of Rick about her—she took very small details and gave them undue significance, all while ignoring larger, more empirically valid data. "We always have to interpret data, that's true, but we should strive to do so without bias." Holly always had the urge to shake her fist at him and say, "I'll show you some bias," but Rick never appreciated this kind of humor, especially the "That's what she said" jokes.

Holly forced herself into a sitting position. She would make some sandwiches, and then she would wait until she had actual evidence before continuing this investigation further. Yes, that is what she would do.

Later that night, as Rick lay in bed reading an issue of *Wired* magazine, Holly considered how to broach the topic. If she could get Rick on her side, they could present a united front against Tina, root out the truth.

"Have you noticed anything weird about Tina?"

"Like what?" Rick continued reading.

"I don't know…" Holly hoped Rick would search his memory and find some image that, upon further consideration, was out of the ordinary. She hoped he could hold it up, this creaking, burnished thing, for both of them to examine together.

Rick flipped the page to an article on Japanese robots with artificial intelligence. Holly could see the creepy, almost-lifelike faces and wondered, briefly, if her husband were a robot, would she be able to tell?

"She has a new imaginary friend. She named him Peepers."

"Mmm."

"I think he's based on our neighbor, Frank. You know, the man who drives the school bus? Don't you think that's a little weird?"

"What's so weird about it? She sees him every day."

"Yes, but how does she see him? That's the question."

Rick set the magazine down on the bed. "If you have something you want to talk about, Holly, just say it."

"I think this man may be molesting our daughter." The words felt sharp, like spitting out glass.

"Shit, Holly. Where did this come from?"

"She keeps talking about going to secret places with him. Alone."

"Frank?"

"No, Peepers."

"Jesus Christ." Rick picked up his magazine and then put it down again. "That's the whole point of an imaginary friend. They're imaginary. I.e. not real."

"I know that," Holly said, "But what if he's actually a stand-in for a real person? What if Tina's trying to tell us something through Peepers?"

"And what evidence do you have to support this theory?"

There it was, those brick-hard words that slammed every conversation still. "Well…"

"So what you're saying is, you want me to go accuse our neighbor of something horrific based on a hunch?"

"No."

"Oh, hello, Frank. Lovely weather we're having, isn't it? By the way, did you happen to molest my daughter recently?"

"Rick, knock it off. This isn't funny."

"Damn right it isn't funny. Next time you want to give me a heart attack with some insane accusation, please have something tangible to back it up."

Rick picked up the magazine and held it close to his face, as though he could block out both Holly and their conversation. Holly flipped onto her side, angry at both Rick and herself for thinking this could go any other way. It was a long time before she fell asleep, running over every detail of the past few days, hoping to find something she had overlooked, some tiny piece of shrapnel she could lob at Rick and say, "Here, see? Now who's being ignorant?"

The siren-wail began around 2am, a high-pitched sound with pitches and swells and a brief, loaded quiet before beginning again. It took Holly a moment to recognize the sound of her daughter crying. She turned to Rick, who was lying perfectly still, his chest rising and falling so rhythmically she knew he must be faking. She threw back the covers and stumbled to Tina's room.

It took a moment for Holly's eyes to adjust. She saw, first, the heap of toys strewn around the bed, then the bureau with the doily runner her mother had insisted upon and the jewelry box filled not with rings or necklaces but with rocks from each neighbor's driveway, and finally, the lump of Little Mermaid bedspread half-covering an oval-shaped wet spot.

"Honey." Holly touched the twitching lump of bedspread. "It's okay. It happens."

Tina flung the bedspread to reveal a mass of tangled, static-y bed-head that would have been funny in any other circumstance. "I had a nightmare."

"Oh, sweetheart, I'm sorry. Why don't you hop up so we can get you cleaned up?"

"I was swimming in the ocean and there was a shark and his teeth were so big and he was coming and I tried swimming away but I couldn't move and he was coming towards me and I couldn't move, I tried."

Holly wrapped her arms around the shaking, moist lump that was her daughter. Cool air touched her arms, the hairs on her back. Tina's pink-and-white-sashed window was open. The curtain ruffled and then lay still, as though someone had just brushed past it.

"Sweetheart, did you open the window?"

Tina shook her head. Her sobs grew quiet.

"Then who did?" Holly glanced at the window again, as though it could give her this information. Her heart beat quickly. "Peepers?"

Tina looked up, her face red and puffy. "I tried, Mommy, but the shark was too fast."

Holly ran to the window and shoved her head into the darkness. She scanned their backyard—a wide expanse of dirt and a few clumps of weedy grass. She saw the red and yellow Playskool slide she had meant to take to Goodwill five months ago, and beyond that, the wicker table and chairs she had set up imagining thoughtful conversations at twilight, now covered in a film of dirt and leaves, the wicker curled like beckoning fingers.

Holly closed the window. Her immediate fear, that gut-wringing image of Frank climbing through the window, was preposterous. There was no way a man his size could scale the house, and definitely not without making enough noise to wake her or Rick.

When Holly returned to the bedroom, Rick had pulled the covers up to his chin. The sight filled Holly with such rage, she imagined holding a bullhorn next to his head. Instead, she flicked the overhead light on.

"What," Rick mumbled, "What is it?"

"Tina had a nightmare and wet the bed."

"Oh, okay, I'll be right there." Rick fumbled on the nightstand for his glasses.

"I already took care of it." Holly flicked the light off, throwing everything into sudden darkness. "I just thought you should know."

The next morning, after dropping both kids off at school, Holly did a Google search on nightmares, bedwetting, and lying. On the very first page, under two comment threads and a research paper, she found two articles: "Children and Domestic Violence," and immediately below, "The Psychological Impact of Sexual Assault." Holly felt her breathing go funny, her eyes focus and then stop focusing on the page.

She printed off the second article, the one listing the warning signs of sexual assault. With a thick red marker, she circled Nightmares, Bedwetting, and Lying / Fabrication. She also circled Reluctance to Go to a Particular Place, since Tina had stayed home from school the other day. And who drove the bus to take her to school? The more Holly thought about it, the more the pieces fell into place: incontrovertible evidence.

But there was one more piece of evidence she needed. Frank.

The day moved by slowly, by hours and minutes and seconds. She flipped past trashy reality TV shows and daytime talk shows where privileged hosts tried to trick their guests into revealing some awful secret or childhood trauma for the audience to weep over, safe in their own mundane lives. She tried watching some old 90s shows on the Instant Queue—*X-Files*, *Freaks and Geeks*, *Star Trek: The Next Generation*—but she couldn't keep her mind on it. She would get up, walk a circuit around the house, maybe wash an errant dish, and then sit back down again for a couple minutes before starting the whole process over again. She had already decided to forgo an elaborate dinner. She didn't want to be trapped in the kitchen, chopping an onion or peeling a garlic clove when Frank shuffled up his driveway. So instead she decided that pizza night, usually on Sunday when nobody felt like cooking, would be tonight.

Around three, Holly left to go pick up the kids, feeling a small wedge of guilt at how tedious it was, this shuffling of bodies. Once home, Holly put on *Aladdin*, one of Tina's favorite movies, and left her to sing along to "Friend Like Me." Tyler slunk upstairs to his room, and as Holly watched him go, she noticed his overgrown bangs and his black t-shirt with gothic red lettering. Holly tried to read the words, but too quickly his back was to her. She tried to remember the last time she sat down and talked to Tyler, learned what his interests were, who his friends were. As soon as this business with Tina was resolved, Holly vowed to spend more time with him.

Rick arrived home and she ordered the pizza, all the while keeping watch out the kitchen window. She saw Frank's black Oldsmobile coast past their house, heard the crunch of tires on gravel. She dropped the dish towel she had been using to dry the Tupperware and ran outside, trying to formulate a plan. She jogged up behind Frank, who heaved himself out of the driver's seat with a small groan.

"Hey there," Holly said.

"Oh. Hey." Frank slammed the door shut and looked at Holly, a small wrinkle on his forehead. His cheeks were flushed or sunburned or both.

"How's it going?"

"Good. Just getting home." He looked toward the door as though he could beam himself there by sight alone.

"Oh yeah, me too." Holly wasn't sure why she was lying, but since she had already started, she might as well continue. "Tyler was telling me about this other kid on the bus. Seems to be a real trouble-maker."

"Oh? Which one?"

Holly felt her face go hot. She searched her memory for some kid, any kid, in Tyler's class and came up blank. "I don't remember. He has blonde hair?" Blonde kids were always trouble-makers, in her opinion, cocky Zach Morris wannabes.

"You're thinking of Brandon. He's not that bad, though, just a lotta mouth. Nothing I can't handle, don't you worry." He patted her arm in what he probably imagined was a reassuring fashion.

"Yes. So, out of curiosity, how do you deal with trouble-makers?"

"Oh, well, there are a lot of things I can do." He ran his hand through the receding patch of gray hair shorn close to his head. "I can give 'em assigned seats, I can bring their parents in for a conference."

Holly waited for the rest, but that appeared to be it. "What if a child is really bad, though? Do you kick them off the bus?"

"Nope, can't do that. Wouldn't be safe."

"How about," and here Holly took a breath, tried to slow the furious beat of her heart, "keeping them on the bus after the other kids have gotten off?"

Frank cocked his head to the side like a dog. "What?"

"I mean, what if a kid is really bad? You can't kick them off, but maybe you can keep them on the bus? Drive someplace quiet to give them a good talking to? Just the two of you?"

Frank glanced at his feet, then back at Holly. His eyes squinted as though he were trying to work something out. "Nope, don't do that either." He pulled out his keys. "Listen, it's been nice talking to you, but I should get going. Had a long day, you know."

"Oh, sure, sure. Don't let me keep you."

"All right." Frank began walking toward the house without a wave or goodbye. Holly watched him walk to his front door. Did he fumble with his keys? Did he slam the door shut a little too quickly to hide something she shouldn't see?

Holly walked back to her house. It wasn't enough. She would need something more concrete to bring this man down.

When Holly woke the next morning, it was already 6:30, a full hour later than she meant to sleep. Someone had turned off her alarm.

Downstairs, she heard Tina's screech and Rick's shit-shit-shit. She jogged into the kitchen, where the dishwasher was spewing frothy, bubbly water all over the floor. The bubbles were a dark pink, almost red.

"Did you use the wrong dishwashing liquid?"

"I'm not a goddamn moron, Holly. I didn't even run the damn thing."

Holly glanced at Tina attempting to gather the bubbles in her arms and at Tyler, sunk in a kitchen chair, texting on his phone. When had he gotten a phone? "Did you turn off my alarm?"

"Sorry. I was just trying to give you a break. You've been so stressed out lately…I thought it would be a nice surprise. Guess I went and fucked that up." He looked at his feet as though he were a teenager arriving home past curfew. "They missed the bus, you know."

Holly felt a brightness in her chest, brief and illuminating. She wrapped her arms around Rick. "That was very sweet."

He hugged her back, and Holly felt a pinching at the back of her throat. It was rare, her and Rick's bodies occupying the same space, their feelings aimed in the same direction. She could remember staring at his wavy brown hair in her Chaos and Fractals class, a class her friend had convinced her to take to fulfill the college's math requirement, saying "How hard can it be?" Rick had agreed to tutor her, and as they sat in her dorm room, Wal-Mart brand notebooks in their laps, she had marveled at how she could lead his eyes from the graphite-smudged numbers to the strap of her tank top, could lay his body on top of hers without a word. Her body had been his tuning fork. Each time they slept together, he would place a hand on her goose-pimpled skin and listen, alert to subtle changes in her breathing so he could adjust the position of his lips, the movement of his hand. Now, in their king-size bed, neither one leaned towards the other, neither set a frequency for the other to follow.

"Yes, well," she said, straightening herself and gathering her hair behind her ears, "Why don't you head to work and I'll drive the kids to school."

"No, no. I'll drive the kids in. Why don't you deal with this nonsense?"

Holly flipped the latch of the dishwasher and the slopping, whirring motion ground to a stop. "Deal."

After Rick and the kids were gone, Holly gathered a closetful of towels to mop up the water. She clicked open the machine, and it took a second for her eyes to travel past the Corelle dishware to the soggy gray lump beneath the bottom rack. Her eyes saw each detail individually. The fur raised in dark gray clumps. The slashed-open stomach smeared with red. The tiny pink claws curled in prayer or supplication. Holly backed away and wrapped her arms around her stomach. She lifted one foot and then the other as though her body wanted her gone, away from this small dead thing, pounded with water and stabbed with dull kitchen knives.

She remembered the first time Tyler had found a dead animal. When he was four, he had carried a tiny brown sparrow into the living room nestled against his Power Rangers t-shirt. Its eyes were shut and its neck tucked toward its chest. Even worse than the curled claws gripping nothing were the few feathers flipped out at odd angles, all that careful preening throughout its life now worthless. He had held it out for Holly to fix, just as he had for a split seam in Brownie the Bear or a kicked-in Lego house. In response to her son's tears, to that mop of brown hair razed golden by the sun, Holly had set her face stern and told Tyler to take the bird back outside. She warned him of diseases and explained the circle of life, how this bird would feed other, larger animals, like their neighbor's orange and white tabby that Tyler occasionally chased. Though she knew ignoring her son's snot-bubbled face was cruel, it was necessary to toughen him up. Life was cruel, especially to young boys who cried over dead birds.

Holly grabbed a hand towel and picked up the sodden wreck in the dishwasher. She tossed both the mouse and the towel in the trash can. Then she gathered the rest of the towels and flung them into the laundry machine.

As the washing machine pounded the towels clean, Holly climbed the stairs to Tyler's room, the one with the window overlooking Frank's house. She walked past the antique dresser, a present from Rick's mother. Every time Holly opened the drawers to put away underwear and shorts, she was certain the tiny brass handles would rip right off or the delicate ball bearing slides would pop off the track. Underneath Tyler's bed, a twin-size mattress with navy blue sheets, a pile of dirty laundry advanced a little further each day, until Holly gathered a pile to clean, pushing back the tide. For the last several years, there were always various pieces of technology strewn about the room, their mechanical guts exposed. But now all the objects—the old monitor and modem, the transistor radio, the record player—were shoved into corners, completely whole. It was as though he had been tinkering in his workshop for years and then, one day, he had turned the final screw, popped the screen back in place, and was finished. On the bureau she noticed an iPod Touch, the earbuds coiled around the thin blue chrome. She flipped through his song list and discovered bands she had never heard of before—Atreyu, Bullet for my Valentine, Forever the Sickest Kids.

She wrapped the earbuds back around the iPod and set it down on the bureau. As she straightened, some small detail caught her eye. On the side of the bureau, in the top right corner, she saw two small letters carved—LT. Maybe they had been there when Rick's mother had bought the bureau, but Holly doubted it. No, Tyler had carved these letters, most likely initials. There was no heart, no other markings at all, so Holly wasn't sure if this was a best friend, a crush, an enemy. But she knew, looking at the small jagged letters, that he had held a knife to the dark wood in order to strip it away, to make his mark.

Holly straightened. There wasn't time for this now— she had other, more pressing tasks. She glanced out Tyler's window at Frank's house, a pale yellow rancher with rhododendrons circling it. On the bushes, tight purple buds were just beginning to bloom. The driveway was empty, so quickly, before she had time to think about it, Holly was bounding down the stairs and out the door.

She approached the house from the front, glancing behind her every now and again, though it was better to look strong, purposeful, like she had every right to be there. Next to the front steps was a small cartoon frog holding a sunflower. It was such a hideous example of suburbia that it must be a gift. Holly picked it up and slid the panel underneath that she knew would be there. Inside was a spare key. Frank seemed the type of man who, if a woman told him the proper way to do something, would immediately oblige.

Holly looked at the key nestled in her palm. There was a line, and that line was the front door. If she crossed it, she would be breaking the law, something she had never done before, except when she had stolen a poinsettia from her college's main administrative building right before Christmas break. But that didn't really count.

But if she was right about Frank, he hadn't just crossed a line, he had crossed an entire goddamn ocean. There was no coming back for him.

She slid the key into the lock and opened the door.

Inside the kitchen, she expected to find a sink full of dirty dishes, perhaps a few flies swarming an overflowing trash can, but the whole place was tidy. A long line of battered wooden cabinets and an electric stovetop that looked brand new stood above a grayish-white linoleum floor. Holly kicked herself for not doing more research before coming here. She had no idea what sort of man a child molester was. Did they keep a pristine house or were they slobs? Should she be on the lookout for an obsessive collection or the absence of any knickknacks? Inside the cabinets were a few mismatched pots and pans, and then a long expanse of wood before a single ant trap. If she opened the fridge, she would find some condiments and take-out containers, maybe a single block of cheese. The freezer would contain several frozen dinners. Obviously, the kitchen was not the right place.

The living room housed a black leather sofa and matching La-Z-Boy recliner, the leather creased and flattened. A small Toshiba television sat on top of a TV tray, and Holly wondered if Frank had misunderstood the term entirely.

She peeked under the sofa and recliner, but there was nothing there either. Similar to the kitchen, the living room was tidy—no piles of unread magazines, no tipped-over soda cans, no castaways at all (an ugly souvenir mug, a single unwashed sock, a water-logged trivia book en route from one bathroom to another).

The trash! Why hadn't Holly thought of that earlier? If this was a man who kept a clean house, then the most incriminating evidence would be thrown away. She dashed into the kitchen and lifted the stained white lid of the trash can, wishing immediately she had the foresight to bring gloves. She grabbed a paper towel from the counter and began to gently move each item. There were a few plastic trays with the last dregs of peas or green beans congealed in the corner, some cans of Natural Light, a sliced-open package for headphones, and what looked like an entire potato just beginning to sprout.

Holly straightened and replaced the lid of the trash can, tossing the paper towel inside. She walked through the kitchen and the living room and stopped before a long, blank hallway. The walls were bare and scuffed gray where someone had slammed into them, hard, before moving towards the bedroom.

Holly checked her watch: almost noon. She considered walking back to her house, making some lunch, and coming back later, but she knew this was just her stalling, desperate to escape the buzzing whine of panic flitting through her head.

She walked down the hallway and turned the brass-colored door knob. A puff of gathered heat hit her in the face. Inside were rumpled yellow sheets, a comforter balled at the foot of the bed. She wished she had brought a blacklight to run over the sheets like in *CSI*, but there was no way to tell one person's bodily fluid from another, not without a full forensics team. She inched into the room, toed the heaps of dirty laundry cast around the bed into smaller piles. They were all man-sized: collared shirts and trousers and an occasional pit-stained undershirt. In the corner, on a fold-out card table, sat a laptop. It was an old brick-style Dell, and when she booted it up, her fingers hovering over the keyboard, it whirred and whirred like something close to death. After several aching minutes, it loaded a photo of snow-covered mountains, probably one of the backgrounds that came with the computer.

The only shortcuts on the menu were for Internet Explorer and Help and Support, so she started to run some searches. First, child pornography, and then just porn. Nothing. He wouldn't label his folders something so obvious. She tried children, then child, then secret. Finally, she tried Tina's name. Nothing came up. Holly knew she should go through his browser history, but she wasn't sure how to do that (another reason to be better prepared). Instead, she double-clicked My Pictures and found a single folder named Photographs.

"That's a little redundant," she muttered to herself to still the frantic thrumming in her chest.

She put all twenty-two photos on a slideshow, one of the few things she did know how to do. Each photo was a different location around town. She recognized the dirt and gravel walkway of the park, the concrete bear enclosure at the zoo, the carousel in the mall food court, the Shorebirds field, the Delmarva Oil plant across the water, a random sycamore tree. Was the tree from their neighborhood? Difficult to tell. In over half of the pictures there were children, sometimes the focus of the shot, as in the case of the carousel, and sometimes not, a blurred-out face in the corner, pointing at the bears.

Holly watched the slideshow three times before finally clicking it off. It wasn't enough. Yes, there were children, and yes, they weren't his, but there was nothing inappropriate about the photos. Creepy, yes. Inappropriate, no. He might just be an amateur photographer.

The front door slammed closed. Holly wondered briefly if someone else was breaking in, and then realized it was Frank. He was a bus driver—of course he would come home for lunch. She whispered "Shit-shit-shit" and then put a hand over her mouth. She pressed the power button until the screen clicked off. No sense going through a long and potentially loud shutdown process. She tiptoed to the bedroom door and closed it just as she heard feet sounding down the hall.

Her eyes blurring with panic, she looked around the room. The bed was too low for her to crawl under. That just left the closet. She tucked herself in a gap of empty hangers and closed the door. For a moment, she felt like she was in a movie. She had the impression that if Frank found her, he would kill her. As she heard the door open and bedsprings creak, she assured herself at most he would be confused and angry. Definitely not homicidal.

For several minutes, it was completely quiet. Then, Frank shifted on the bed and Holly could hear a quiet depression of buttons, as though he was dialing a phone. She imagined one of those giant cordless phones with the long collapsible antenna from the 90s. It would certainly match the rest of the décor.

"Hey sis. Fine, fine, how are you?"

Holly strained to hear the sister's responses through the phone, but she could only hear Frank.

"Yeah, I know."

—

"I can visit her next weekend. Nobody expects you to do everything."

—

"That sounds just like her. Still full of piss and vinegar."

—

"It's the same. Kids get on, kids get off."

—

"Yeah, they're still doing it. You know how it is. Kids will be kids."

—

"At this point, I can do their lines for them. 'Hey fatty, why are you so fat? Did you eat the last bus driver? Are you poor? Too poor to buy new shirts? How much money do you make, tubbo? Enough for some fried chicken? Some KFC, motherfucker?'"

—

"Yeah, I did that."

—

"Did that too. The mothers don't believe their goddamn angels even know how to say motherfucker. You know how much Cynthia hates me, so she sides with them. Gives their precious little darlings another chance."

—

"Actually, I saw one of the moms yesterday. Walked right up to me."

—

"You know she wouldn't believe me. Wanted to know about some kid bullying her kid. Didn't tell her her little shit is right in the thick of it with the rest of 'em."

—

"Last I heard some other districts were getting cameras. No dumb bitch with a stick up her ass could argue with me then."

—

"Maybe I will. Or maybe I'll just wring their scrawny little necks. Ain't no cameras on the bus. Who's gonna know?"

—

"Yeah, yeah, I know. I will."

—

"Love you too. Take care, sis."

He hung up the phone and rolled off of the bed. "Nobody would fucking know," he said again as he walked out of the bedroom, shutting the door behind him. Holly peeked out of the closet. The room was empty.

She would need to hear the front door close before she could leave the room, so she sat on the floor of the closet and waited. Was Tyler a bully now? That seemed to be the gist of what Frank was saying. She tried to imagine Tyler on the bus with a group of green-haired punks taunting Frank, but she couldn't. She kept picturing him with a pair of oversized glasses, taking apart a transistor radio in his room, the exquisite precision of each screw and gear laid bare. She laid her head against the back of the closet. She would have to address this before Tyler got a beating from Tubby. For a moment, Holly wondered if that was how it happened: you thought of a person as his nickname, Fatty or Tubby, and it became easier to justify. It wasn't ridicule; it was simply an observation, more or less fact. Maybe, given enough time, you thought you were helping the person, acting as a mirror for the stomach rolls, the double-chin. And when that same groaning bulge cranked open the doors, day after day, you began to think he deserved it. After all, you had warned him, alerted him to his own corpulence. Continuing to hunker down against your insults was his choice now, wasn't it?

Holly cracked her knuckles, and remembering she was still in hiding, placed her palms on the ground. Was this her and Rick's fault for making fun of Frank? No, she wasn't a bully. She recalled her earlier conversation with Frank: beyond the insinuation that he was a child molester, she had been very polite. Besides, what Tyler did was different—a purposeful cruelty. She never tried to hurt Frank's feelings, and if anything had gotten back to him, it was an accident. Holly crossed her arms and rested her head on her knees, trying to keep her stomach from doing, as Tina would say, "the flippity flops."

Holly picked Tyler and Tina up from school, she supposed for the last time. There was no evidence to support the idea that Frank was a child molester. The itchy, leftover details—the meticulous house, the pictures of children—Holly let slide to the back of her mind, behind last week's grocery list. Now that she had exonerated him through her brief turn as spy, she felt more comfortable saying or even thinking those words. Before, the lip-pucker of "mo" and the teeth-baring hiss of "lest" would have caused a full-body quiver. Now, it was just a word, an unfortunate story on the evening news concerning someone else's child.

As Holly examined Tyler's black t-shirt in the rearview mirror, finally sussing out the word Atreyu, Tyler looked up from his phone. "What?"

Holly motioned towards his shirt. "What kind of band is that? Rock?"

Tyler shrugged. "Punk, I guess."

"Do you like it?"

Tyler shrugged again. Holly waited for a sure, or a nah, or a shut the hell up, even, but Tyler said nothing.

"When your father gets home, we have something we would like to discuss with you."

"Ooh, trouble trouble, you're in trouble!" Tina squealed.

"Whatever."

Holly could have grilled Tyler in the car or when they got home, but she had already had a long, difficult day, and it would be easier with Rick. Truthfully, she was frightened to confront this sudden leap into teenager-dom—the stoic apathy, the casual cruelty.

When Rick arrived home, Holly grabbed his arm and pulled him into the house. "We have a problem."

"Can I set my briefcase down first?"

Holly touched his arm, hoping to transmit her knowledge from that afternoon. She walked to the bottom of the stairs. "Tyler, come down here!"

Tyler thumped down the stairs and flopped onto the couch. He continued moving his thumbs over the keypad.

"Put the phone away, please."

Tyler sighed and put the phone in his pocket. He pushed a stockinged toe against the coffee table.

"Your father and I need to speak to you about something. We know you've been bullying the bus driver, Frank."

Rick turned to Holly. "What?"

"You and all your hooligan friends. You call him fatty and tubby and ask if he wants to eat KFC. And you say he's poor."

Rick looked from Holly to Tyler. Tyler kept his eyes on the floor. His big toe flexed against the lip of the coffee table.

"Don't try to deny it. I have proof."

"What proof?" Rick crossed his arms.

Holly wanted to grab Rick by the throat—they were supposed to be interrogating Tyler together, but Rick was acting like his goddamn defense attorney.

"One of your friends, uh"—Holly thought back to her last conversation with Frank and suddenly remembered—"Brandon. He told his parents and they told me."

The secret to lying, Holly realized, was simply having enough information.

"Is this true, Tyler?" Rick asked.

Tyler sighed and kept his eyes on the ground. "Maybe. I dunno. It was their idea." He shrugged.

"I'm going to the kitchen to defrost the fish for tomorrow. When I come back, I want an explanation. And it better be good." Holly recognized how ludicrous this demand was. How could Tyler have any reasonable explanation beyond peer pressure or hormones, the body suddenly growing beyond its old desires? She imagined Rick taking a cross-section of his brain and cataloguing every new thought that sparked into life. Maybe then they could keep up with him, understand the subtle nuances between one scowl and the next.

Holly walked into the kitchen and opened the freezer. Beside the ice cube tray and bag of individually frozen filets were her wallet and keys. Both items were covered in ice crystals.

"That's one way to keep your cool." Rick stood beside her and grinned.

"Wow."

"Seriously, though, why are your wallet and keys in the freezer?"

"Why is anything the way it is right now? Did you know about Tyler and the other kids on the bus?"

"Of course not. I don't really know anything about him lately. He stopped wanting to dig through old electronics at garage sales a couple months ago, and last month, he stopped taking things apart altogether. And then, he wanted a Droid and I thought he was back, good old Tyler. But he just wanted to text his friends." Rick ran his hand through his hair. "Do you see the shit he's wearing? And now he's bullying the bus driver? Who the fuck is in my living room? I just don't know anymore."

Holly removed her ice-encrusted wallet, a knock-off from Walgreens. She touched a cluster of ice crystals, their tiny, beautiful pattern perfectly explainable through science, the molecules shifting and realigning. Yet within each delicate shape was a mystery, a hidden pattern beyond a fourth grade science class. Holly didn't know what it was, but as she touched the pointed tendrils, she could feel the mystery hum inside her, electric. They melted on her fingertips.

"Is Tyler in trouble?" Tina looked up with eyes just a little too innocent.

Holly decided to try one last time. She squatted until she was eye-level with Tina and pointed to the freezer. "You didn't do this?"

"It was Peepers."

Holly glanced toward the living room where Tyler was silently slumped on the couch. "Honey, is Peepers actually Tyler?"

"No." Tina covered her face with her hands, then peeked through her fingers. Her voice dropped to a whisper. "Peepers is a ghost."

"A ghost," Rick chuckled. "She certainly has an imagination. Ready?"

"Why not?" As Holly readied herself for the dramatic sighs and maudlin excuses, to hand out a punishment that would quickly become the norm, she imagined her children on the yellow bus as it floated into the sky: Frank a pale, ghostly image at the wheel, Tina and Tyler waving once before their faces leeched all color, until they too were specters, their bodies pointed to the wine-dark sky, ready to blast open the secrets of the universe, one flaming gas-ball at a time.

GRADE A

The chickens are coming down the line. Feet bound, neck slit, they head into the Blood Room. Frank, one of the line supervisors, always calls it the Little Hall of Horrors. I chuckle every time (though it's barely clever) in a desperate desire to bond. His crisp smile's a signal to get fucked. I get it—my job is bondage: hold him to the line, hold him to the work. His fiesta boys do something dumb, I have to write him up. Merits, demerits, all that horseshit.

Halfway into the Blood Room stands Tyrone, the only black guy in the place, wearing a yellow rain slicker and gripping a meat cleaver between crossed arms. He waits for any bird that's made it through the electric bath and spinning blade intact. Alive. He's supposed to stand with arms at his sides, but even I'm not dumb enough to write him up. He gives me a curt nod that I return. I tap one two three four five six seven eight nine ten times on the clipboard, enough to reach the end.

By the end of my shift, my white shoes and my white lab coat are covered in blood. It reminds me of that "Out, damned spot" scene from *Macbeth*, except it's different for me. I don't even notice the blood.

I look down at my checklist, though there's no need. No gaps between the chickens coming down the line. No chicken parts cluttering the floor. (The rats can grow as big as lap dogs here.) In another twenty minutes, make sure maintenance washes the blood to the grates lining the far wall. In another thirty, pull ten more chickens from the line.

Next up, the de-feather machine. I call it the Plucker, though a better name would be the Thrasher. After that, the dismemberment room.

A week after I earned my Bachelor's in English, Film Studies concentration, I grabbed a Shore Stop paper and spread it on the once-white Formica table. When was the last time I held a real newspaper? I couldn't recall.

I opened to the Help Wanted section and circled every job requiring a college degree. I used a red Sharpie, thick point, and tried to make my circles the same as those stock image photos—an almost-perfect oval, the end never fully closed. You can tell the circle-drawer is rushed, scouring pages and pages of classifieds, and yet the perfect imprecision also signals a kind of trepidatious excitement. Maybe this job, finally, is the one.

Making that perfect circle is tough. Try too hard and it winds up shaky, uncertain, more of a question than a statement. Just like my mother's hands my senior year of high school. When I held out the permission form she had to sign to accept my scholarship to UMES, the paper shook like an accusation. You deserve this? I had no idea why I had gotten any scholarship, let alone a full ride. My grades were okay, mostly Bs and Cs with a couple of As in subjects like history and art. Nothing worthy of notice. Maybe because I was white? I found the paper later that week, crumpled where her hand had gripped it, beneath a pile of magazines, several scratched frames with the stock photo still inside, and a colander with drooping pasta still mashed into the holes. I forged her signature, my hand shaking from something, and it almost looked right.

One of the jobs I circled was for Quality Assurance at the local chicken plant. No experience required! I wondered what they'd make of my degree. Another Hitchcock-wannabe? Or some spoiled white boy cooking up Daddy's cash? The truth is even worse.

I don't really talk to the line workers. They're all Mexican, and they don't speak much English. Maybe some of them are another nationality, Puerto Rican or something, but I'm no expert. I just call them all Paco. Maybe that sounds racist. I'd be surprised, though, if they could tell the difference between us white guys.

Today Paco #1 is speaking his tickety-tickety Spanish to Paco #3 as they hang chickens on the line. Who knows what they're saying? Maybe they're saying shit behind your back, or maybe they're complaining about the work, or maybe they're just reminiscing about the pussy back in Mexico City. Only one of them looks any different from the others, a real Casanova-looking motherfucker with slicked-back hair and high cheekbones. He's taller than the others too, and quieter. In my head, I call him Fajita Fabio. Sometimes I get the urge to push my finger into his chest and tell him all the ways he's fucked. I don't know why. But while the other guys occasionally break code, he never so much as breathes funny.

And then, as if to illustrate my point, Paco #1 grabs a chicken that's making a break for the wall and throws it at Paco #3. Paco #2 squeezes the chickens until a geyser of shit erupts from them. Paco #3 grabs the chicken that Paco #1 threw and punts it like a football. It arcs in a glory of beak and feathers before landing on the other side of the room.

Frank isn't there, which is another point I'll have to dock him for later, so it's up to me to stop this nonsense.

"Hola!" I yell, and then, "Vamonos!"

They stop what they're doing, which is going to cause breaks in the line and more docked points. Mouths parted, eyes wild, they stare. For a moment, I wonder what would happen if they all charged me at once. How would it feel to succumb to those chicken-rough hands? Then, as though nothing has happened, they begin hanging birds again.

They wear the same white coat as me, but mine has my name stitched on the pocket and theirs doesn't. Like that's the only way we're different.

The first time we knew something was wrong was my junior year of high school. Mom had poured an entire pot of boiling water onto the floor. She was still wearing her work shoes, all leather and whorls, instead of the bear-footed slippers, bought at a yard sale last August, that would soon become her feet.

"I don't know what came over me," she said when Sam and I came down the stairs. "I could have sworn the sink was right there." She pointed to the kitchen table.

Steam rose off of the water with the quiet insistence of a summer storm. I recalled our childhood game where we pretended the floor was hot, lava-slick, so we slid from the couch to the loveseat to our father's favorite chair. (Even after he left, we still considered it his.)

We reached across the boiling sheen to grab our mother's hand. The water seeped across the linoleum and coated the living room carpet. Noodles slipped through the water in gestures both beautiful and obscene.

Mom's hand shook as she touched her forehead. She pulled it away as if expecting something there.

"I need to pay more attention. Someone could have gotten hurt."

If you're Mexican and want to learn English or you're white and want to learn Spanish, the company supports your endeavors to better yourself. They do this through a woman named Marigold. She teaches all the language courses and has a studious look about her, though she doesn't wear glasses. Perhaps it is her long, thin nose or her curly red hair perpetually tied back. Perhaps it is her voice with the soft incandescence of a Bunsen burner.

I saw her one day in a small white room filled with Mexicans. She pointed to a phrase on the whiteboard that said, "I am very pleased to meet your acquaintance."

Is that what we teach every foreigner, I wondered, how to be cold and overly formal? How forever to be outside? It occurred to me then why Felipe, one of the few Mexicans who climbed the corporate ladder to line supervisor, who insisted that we call him Philip, always spoke with such formality. "What a beautiful day this is, the second day of October." Good morning to you too, Philip.

One glassy fall day, the windows hoar-filmed and sour, I knew it was time. Speak, muse, I murmured, though I couldn't remember where that was from. Shakespeare? As good a muse as any.

"Marigold," I said, though my voice cracked, so it sounded more like "-anyload."

She looked up, startled, from a desk full of papers. Did employees who chose these classes still have homework?

"Yes, hello?" She narrowed her eyes, then widened them in feint warmth. "I'm sorry, I didn't see you! You startled me."

"Mike," I said, to alleviate her discomfort.

"Of course. What can I do for you?"

She reminded me of my elementary school librarian, a woman with big tits and a low-cut blouse who would clasp her hands together, lean over the desk, and ask me what I most wanted to see. "It might just be in a book," she would whisper through soon-parted lips. Later, I would think she single-handedly started the whole "sexy librarian" trend. At the time, I just knew I really really really wanted to read more Berenstain Bears.

"I was wondering about the Spanish classes," I said. "Is there a lot of homework?"

She shuffled her papers as if caught doing something wrong. "I don't like to call the assignments homework. It's such a pejorative term. Instead, I like to think of them as enhanced learning experiences."

I nodded, though it was bullshit. "I know exactly what you mean."

She smiled, and it was radiant, like sunflowers in bloom or an atomic bomb. I wanted to know how to say in Spanish "Your smile holds the heat of a thousand suns burning in my soul." I thought of all the things I would do for her, like listen to an entire Joni Mitchell album or get up early on a Saturday to attend a farmer's market.

"Sh—Sh—Sh—Sh—Shall we go?" a voice from the doorway said.

I turned and saw Scotty, a line supervisor with a moustache and stutter. Just one would be a significant deterrent, but two?

"Of course," Marigold said with a blush. She linked her arm in Scotty's, and he gave me a look halfway to swagger.

They walked off together, arm in arm. I haven't spoken to her since.

Mom's staying at Sam's place in Alexandria for two days. It's actually the apartment of her boyfriend Trevor, a project manager for DC Water and Sewer she met at

Fager's Island. She can do better. He still owns a pager for Christ's sake.

With the house to myself, Paul and Jeanette come over. Her name isn't Jeanette anymore, though. Now she wants to be called Anka. Get it? Paul and Anka. Yeah, I didn't think it was that funny, either.

We all met in a Film Noir class our Sophomore year of college. We discussed *The Big Heat* with voices nasally and pretentious. Six months later, both Paul and Jeanette dropped out, and four months after that, they both enrolled at the local community college. Jeanette was going to pursue Nursing until she took her first Anatomy & Physiology course. They both graduated with degrees in General Studies and Jeanette changed her name. Now Paul works as a shift manager at Food Lion and Anka works at the Gap.

Paul brings over some kine bud, and we smoke it in my old college bong. He complains about the women on food stamps and how they can never suss out what products are covered. "It's not that fucking hard, man, but they act like it takes a goddamn rocket scientist to figure out. And then they back up my line jabbing fingers at the booklet like I'm the one who can't fucking read."

He takes a long hit, pauses, then slowly lets it out. "I mean, I try to be patient. Everyone has to eat. But sometimes I wonder if they have to be such cunts about it."

Anka gets really high, really fast, and starts walking around and touching things.

"Hey, how much free shit do you get?" She grabs my company jean jacket, wraps the arms around her, and then flops into the company lawn chair.

"A few things." I don't mention the company water bottle in the dishwasher or the company duffel bag in the closet. Last Thanksgiving, I got a free turkey. Sam spends holidays with Trevor's family now, so last Thanksgiving was just Mom and me. I bought some boxed stuffing and boxed mashed potatoes and canned cranberry sauce to go with the turkey.

"Happy Thanksgiving," I told Mom as I sat her at the table.

"Your father always forgets to lock the car door."

I nodded. No real response was needed.

Mom dipped her finger in the mashed potatoes and slid it on her tongue. I realized then I forgot the butter. "It isn't right," she said. Her eyes were curved and wet. "Michael will be so upset with me." I cleared off the dishes and made us peanut butter and jelly sandwiches. She peeled apart the slices of bread and ate them one at a time.

Paul and Anka don't talk for a while, and it's nice, having bodies so close without having to speak. Sometimes I think life would be a lot better if everyone was high all the time.

"Hey, I was just wondering." Anka sticks her hand between the plastic slats. She rolls her fingers right, then left. "Do we only eat girl chickens? Or do we eat boy chickens too?"

"Roosters," Paul says. "Boy chickens are roosters."

"Yeah, roosters. Do we eat them?"

"Roosters aren't fattened with antibiotics the same way hens are. We probably produce more hens when they're in egg form."

"But how do you, like, choose whether you get a boy or a girl?"

"Something to do with light…and heat." Paul smacks his lips and looks at me. In addition to drying his mouth, kine bud takes away his narcissistic faith.

I shrug. "They don't look much like chickens or roosters by the time they get to me."

"Eww, gross," Anka says, "How can you still eat chicken after working there?"

"You get used to it."

"Does it smell bad?"

Yes, it smells bad, I tell her, but just like the blood, you get used to it.

Anka gasps, and I lean forward in case the bud is having a bad effect. "Does the cafeteria serve chicken?"

I sigh. They serve chicken nuggets and burgers and salad. But I don't usually eat there. Eating there would emphasize just how few friends I have in the plant. How none of the line supervisors want a QA at their table. How not even the other QA in my section, a woman with heavy lines from too much sun or smoking or both, a woman who is overly dull and overly formal at the same time, wants me at her table.

"Where do you eat, then?"

"McDonalds, usually. But there's a whole strip of fast food places on Rt. 1, so I switch it up."

"Do you get the Chicken McNuggets?"

"Sometimes," I say, and then, "It's just meat," to forestall her next inevitable question. But the first time I ordered the nuggets, and this was mainly to prove to myself that I could, I sat at the small plastic table, surrounded by families. I opened the cardboard container, the flaps clicking out of place, and breathed in the scent of grease-fried meat. For a moment, I hovered above my body—my vision tilted to the right, click, click, and it was weird and foreign and unnameable, I was myself and not myself, the chicken was food and not food, and even the word *chicken* sounded strange, and this whole meat eating business was like those monks who self-immolate in protest, full of sound and fury, but signifying nothing. And then a toddler screamed and I was back, staring at the exact same Value Meal as before. I ate the chicken and the fries and the coke. Then I cleared the remainder into the trash, placed my plastic tray on the trash can, and drove back to work.

Actually, that part about the smell isn't true. You never get used to the smell. When I first stepped out of the car, my resume tucked neatly into a folder, it reached into my nose and throat and squeezed.

Ever since that first day, I've tried to think of a way to describe it, but there isn't a word or phrase that can touch it. It's not simple, like blood, which is just the smell of rotten pennies. It isn't the smell of animal fear, either, which is mostly sweat and saliva. It's not the Mexicans, who shower every other month, as far as I can tell, and leave shit-covered toilet paper in the corners of the stalls. It's not even the viscera of a newly disemboweled chicken. It's all of those things forging themselves into something new and terrible, an active presence that ebbs and flows through the plant like the smoke monster from *Lost*. It makes you feel awful, deep in your still-beating heart. It is knowing that something is deeply, terribly wrong, and there is not a goddamn thing you can do about it.

I began buying more fragrant shampoos and body washes. Before it was just water and Dial soap, but now I use the special Paul Mitchell Tea Tree shampoo and conditioner along with the Nivea for Men Hair and Body wash. I step out of the shower and am bathed in spice and scent. It is both invitation and armor. Musk and mask. Most importantly, though, it is not the smell of the chicken plant.

When I received the full scholarship, my sister and I sat down at the kitchen table. Mom was getting worse. She was starting to misplace files and write down the wrong appointment times at Dr. Paternawicz's office. She had a second job cleaning houses, and we both worried about her lugging the heavy vacuum cleaner up and down the stairs. At home, random crap was piling on the couch and table and loveseat. Bills were paid late, if at all.

I knew I had to be the one to say it. "Maybe an assisted living facility?"

"Yeah, great," Sam said. "Thanks for raising us, Mom, now get lost. She's not even fifty yet."

"It's the most realistic option," I said. I tried to sound as calm and rational as possible, though the thought of Mom in one of those death factories made me want to tear out my own skin. I wondered, not for the first time, what Dad would have done.

Sometimes when I thought about him, I pictured Arnold Schwarzenegger with one arm over Jamie Lee Curtis in her little black dress, shooting the Arab terrorists. Then I pictured Jamie Lee Curtis in her strip scene, and that was no good. I couldn't get a handle on Dad's face anymore, so he morphed into Schwarzenegger or Van Damme. When I pictured Dad leaving, he was usually Tom Hanks. He grabbed two large suitcases and told Mom (in this scene, Julia Roberts) that it was for the best.

He could never be the father we all deserved. Sometimes, though, he would morph back into himself, a man with thinning hair and a light grey suit. Then I would imagine myself at the top of the stairwell, my hand depressing a lever, and my father exploding in a thousand shards before he could get away.

"I have an idea," my sister said. "I've been thinking this over, and I think it will work."

She outlined a plan in which she would forge a letter quitting Mom's job at the office. Then she would go with Mom to clean houses. All the while she would keep her job as a waitress at Famous Dave's BBQ. And when Mom got really bad, she would hire in-home help.

"What about school?"

She shrugged. "I'm failing all my classes anyway. I'd have to repeat junior year."

"All your classes?"

"Ugh, you sound like Mr. Hemery. 'You need to buckle down, young lady, or you'll wind up on the streets.' Buckle this," she said, flipping an imaginary guidance counselor the bird. "It's so fucking tedious. The Battle of Gettysburg, sines and cosines, cellular mitosis. I mean, who fucking cares? There's so much real shit going on in the world. It's like, open your eyes. This stuff is useless."

She continued on with her plan. I would attend school for four years, at which point I'd have a college degree. Then I'd get a full-time job and take over the bills and Mom's care while Sam pursued her career.

"And what will your career be?"

"I don't know! I haven't figured it out yet."

"Without a high school diploma?"

"I'll get my GED. It's not like it's hard, it's just boring."

"And then, what? I take care of Mom for the rest of my life?"

"No, dummy. In four years I'll be settled, and we'll trade off or something."

I knew what I needed to do. I needed to call someone from social services. I needed an adult with experience. I couldn't leave it in the hands of my kid sister.

Later that week, I tried to get Mom to sign off on my scholarship. Then I forged her signature.

That same week, Sam gathered all the random piles of crap and threw them all away. She rolled the trash out on Sunday. She ran the dishwasher and put away the dishes.

She ran the vacuum. She cleaned the bathroom, even the shit-stained can.

I promised I would help out whenever I could.

Sam flipped her hand, her hair held back in a bandana. "I can handle it. And if I need someone to do the heavy lifting, I'll call Sean."

I tried to envision leather-jacket clad Sean fixing a busted water pipe. I couldn't.

"Four years," Sam said. "Study hard, bro."

My Senior year, I took a Feminism in Film class. I was running out of film classes to take, and I figured this would be a good place to meet chicks. Boy was I wrong. If ever there was a group of women with a chip on their shoulder, professor included, this was it. Every girl with daddy issues who came out zealot instead of harlot was in that room. We talked about the male gaze, voyeurism, female spectators, and the patriarchy, always the patriarchy. The problem was that I'd already seen most of the movies. *Rear Window* I'd seen five or six times. I'd even seen *Peeping Tom* before. I wanted a movie to erode my caked-on armor of scorn, something to make the classroom go blurry and faint.

At night, I'd flop on the couch while my sister flipped from one reality show to the next. I'd update her on my classes and she'd update me on Mom. As the years passed, her body slipped to the contours of the couch with greater necessity and ease. She'd mmm hmm when I told her about my professors or the funny thing Paul did in class last Tuesday.

"Sounds fun," she'd say. "Yesterday I pulled a hairball the size of a weiner dog out of some woman's shower drain."

"I can quit," I'd say, feeling guilt squeeze my chest.

"No, no," she'd say. "This is your time. Just remember, three more years."

She started leaving notes tacked to my door: a list of chores, phone calls to make. At the end of each note was a countdown. Twenty-four more months, twenty-three more months, twenty-two, twenty-one…

Near the end of class we watched the adaptation of *Beloved* with Oprah Winfrey. I never read *Beloved* or any black stories. It wasn't intentional; I just never really cared.

We all watched the movie. I wondered what Sam would do if there was a poltergeist haunting our house. I imagined Sam's thin arms around Mom the same way

Sethe holds her children in the tool shed. I imagined Sam considering what she must do, the weight that will settle in her arms and neck and chest.

At the end of the film, Paul D says, "You your best thing, Sethe."

And then, I burst into tears. Not a single stoic tear rolling down my cheek, either. This was some serious weeping, sticky nose goop and heavy gasping and everything. It was not a pretty sight. And you know what? Not one of those fucking bitches said a damn word. Not "it's okay," not "there, there," not even a goddamn pat on the shoulder. Where'd all their feminism go? Was it all just an excuse to sit around, watch movies, and bullshit, just like the rest of us?

The film ended and the lights stayed off. I stopped crying. The professor started to ask a question and trailed off. She let us out early.

The director of Quality Assurance has started cross-training me. Today I'm in the part of the plant where they package the chickens. One machine cuts the chicken into parts: breast, legs, thigh. Another machine strips the skin, removes the bones, and stretches the new, taut plastic over the boneless breasts. In another part of the plant, whole chickens are dipped into a water tank where they are partially frozen and then shoved into a freezer.

There's a lot less blood here. The chickens look even less like chickens than before. I look at the nice, neat packaging, so familiar from grocery store trips, and don't feel a thing.

The director leads me upstairs to a room with a round oak table. Several men in white coats and colored construction helmets (green for the deboning supervisor, blue for evisceration) sit around the table. I take my place at the one empty spot. It reminds me of the Knights of the Round Table, except I guess we're more like Grim Reapers.

I know what this means. They're getting me ready for promotion. Perhaps they'll make me production supervisor. Or perhaps one of the FDA guys who stops by to "randomly" inspect the plant and give me not-so-secret quizzes will offer me a job.

I have a degree. I have experience now. This could be a career, if I wanted it.

When I drive to pick Mom up from Sam's, Trevor isn't there. Sam's wearing a cable-knit sweater, the kind she would have ridiculed in school. "We gotta put her in a home, Michael."

I can't remember the last time she used my name.

"We can't go on like this."

"We?" I want to ask. Who the fuck is "we"?

"What about your plan?"

Sam looks at me. Her eyes are filmy and wrecked. I wonder how much she actually sees. "I was sixteen when I came up with that. It was a stupid fucking plan."

Mom sits quietly in the backseat of my car. She waits to be driven wherever we are going by the nice young man with the almost-black hair.

"Listen, I did some research." Sam hands me several sheets from assisted living facilities near Mom's house. Her hand shakes, but she steadies it. "Pick the one you think is best. I'll contribute what I can."

On the ride home, Mom does not speak. Some days she tells me stories about myself and Samantha, or about our father. Sometimes her stories make sense, and sometimes the details get mixed up. The last story she told was when I was six and Samantha was seven, and we rolled around the living room over the last fortune cookie. Samantha, she says, was the winner, but only because I could never wring courage from heartache. It doesn't make a lot of sense.

We stop at a red light. It begins raining. Red smears across the windshield in big, angry strokes.

"Your father never hit me," Mom says.

I wait.

"A man shouldn't hit his wife. He should only do nice, loving things."

Fuck. Fuckfuckfuck. I want to scream or hit the steering wheel or crash the car into a telephone pole. Instead, I put the blinker on and turn the car around.

I expected there to be more horror stories when I first started working at the plant. More gruesome accidents and unexplainable events. But there are only a handful, and they're pretty tame. Several maintenance men have lost fingers while cleaning out the machines. A line worker once cracked his helmet with falling debris. Every so often we see a bird wandering around the building and a small, useless part of us roots for it. And then there was Georgie, a line supervisor in the frozen chicken section. The official story is that it was an accident, carelessness rather than fatigue or drugs or booze. The unofficial story, the one that passes in whispers through the line, is different. He was working late one night, 2 or 3am, all by himself. Most of the regular line workers get to leave around midnight while the back end has to finish up. The story goes that he was shutting down the plant after his workers finished freezing the last of the birds. He thought he saw movement in the water tank. When he leaned over to look, a mammoth green claw reached from the water. It was a mutated bird—half chicken, half crocodile. Georgie tried to run, but the giant claw hooked his neck and pulled him in. Some say it is a guardian that watches over the plant. Others say it is vigilante fowl seeking revenge, waiting for the next man to wander off. The truth is that Georgie was probably drunk or high or both. The truth is that someone lowered the temperature of the water tank so it froze over. The truth is that they found him the next morning, his arms and legs curled like a child's, his body preserved in that final position, one neither death nor men with chisels could break.

BABY BLUES

The morning we found the baby growing in our little patch of backyard, nestled snugly between the cluster of ivy and the rhododendron bush the previous tenant had planted, I had tried to broach the subject of finances with Liz without any luck. The way we were currently going, our incoming cash was outflanked by our expenditures, and while I held my own share of the spending, Liz's book fetish was getting a little out of control. While she had always been an avid reader (she was, after all, a part-time English teacher at the local community college with a Master's in Poetry), she normally kept her purchases to one or two books a month, but lately, she had started buying four or five books at a time, sometimes all within a week. Although we weren't yet married or even engaged, we were in a period of transition—a townhouse instead of an apartment, one savings account instead of two—and like all periods of transition, this one teetered between success and disaster.

I had just finished a twelve-hour shift at Telemetry Central in the hospital—a small room filled with monitors that registered heartbeats of all the patients on the cardiac floor. It was my job to monitor those heartbeats, the EKG readings, making sure they stayed within normal range. If they didn't, I would page one of the actual nurses on the floor to check on the patient. I didn't have to deal with any drugs or needles or even leave the room. I just watched those pulsing lines across the screen and let someone know when something went wrong. That was my entire job description. I didn't even need a degree to do this job, just three days of training so I could interpret the rhythms. The worst part wasn't the boredom, though, and it was a boring job. The worst part was that a fatal rhythm, a V-Fib, almost never happened. Instead, a battery would die or a patient would be moved and nobody would tell us. So then I had to page or call the floor and interrupt the nurses from their oh-so-busy schedules, which they were more than happy to inform me of, each and every time. Plus, everyone on the floor was old and had a bad ticker anyway, so when they strained to take a shit, it sometimes made their heart rate spike. At those moments, I had to watch that monitor very carefully, trying to discern when the seconds had ticked away between a really difficult turd and a potentially serious rhythm. Still, it was better than the last job I had working at Home Depot and the job before that, a line cook at the Lighthouse diner.

Not wanting to confront Liz if she was tired from grading essays, I tried to gauge her stress level by walking up behind her and kissing her neck. If she was stressed out, she would pinch her shoulder to her chin and tell me to knock it off. If not, then she would sink her body into the crook of my neck and allow me to support her weight, sometimes even turning up her face to kiss my chin.

But today, she didn't do any of those things. Instead, she turned and faced me, her mouth a thin, tight line with radiating spokes. "You think you're pretty damn funny, don't you?" She pointed to the sliding glass door. Then she stomped up the staircase and slammed the door to our bedroom.

I glanced out into the backyard area, which wasn't a backyard so much as a square of fenced-in brick and a tiny patch of dirt and compost that contained several stick plants, a rhododendron, and a cluster of ivy curling up the fence. And, though I had to look several times, my face pressed up against the glass like a child, there was now a baby growing straight out of the ground. Its little hands clutched at the air, opening and closing onto nothing. From the waist down, it was covered by dirt.

For a while, I didn't do anything but stare at the baby through the glass. There was no way it was an actual baby—it was stuck in the middle of the ground like a plant. Finally, I summoned up my courage, my heartbeat soaring into my chest (at this point, if it was on a monitor, I would be paying attention) and I opened the sliding glass door.

When I reached the baby, I had to push aside the ivy that was threatening to wrap around its waist. I circled the baby three times, peering at it from every angle, trying to figure out if it was a shared hallucination between Liz and me or if it was some kind of robot. If it was the former, it was probably a product of a recent conversation regarding our future. At first, when I told Liz that I definitely wanted children, she had smiled one of those warm, knowing smiles and said that I would make a good father. But lately, when I had broached the subject in terms of the knowable future, she had squeezed the tip of her nose, a gesture that signaled her discomfort, and said she really wasn't entirely sure she wanted children. With a feeling like sinking, I had asked when she had changed her mind and she said she hadn't, only that she had never really thought about it seriously, and anyway, she couldn't think about kids before she had a full-time job and a published chapbook and had been to at least two other countries. When I tried to add up the amount of time it would take for her to accomplish all of these tasks, I had to set aside my calculations as they soared past the seven year mark and disappeared into the ether of the impenetrable future.

So I was left with the possibility that this was some sort of robot baby planted here for God knows what reason. If it was, it was incredibly life-like. There were whisps of hair already forming on its head and tiny creases in its clutching hands. And then, as I leaned down to get an even closer look and finally, irrevocably, touch its feather-soft skin, it grabbed my finger, just like in a movie. I stopped, awestruck, and held perfectly still. The amount of strength it had in its tiny little hand was exactly the amazing amount of strength I always imagined a baby could have.

I don't know how long I crouched there, the baby grasping my finger and staring into my face with a curious expression, but when my legs started to ache and burn, I finally had to loosen his vice-like grip and stand up. The best course of action would probably be to go back inside and call the police. But something in the baby's expression, an unsettling combination of curiosity and trust, made me want to protect him. (I had decided, without having the ability to check, that the baby was a he. Call it gut instinct.) I decided to hold off calling the police until I learned more. Instead, I wandered back inside and started rummaging through the fridge to see if we had any milk.

We only had Liz's soy milk, so I poured that into a cup. With no other way to feed the baby, I plopped down next to the infant, Indian-style, lifted the cup to its tiny, open mouth, and began to very slowly pour the milk in.

At first, the baby gulped the milk down hungrily, and I was pretty proud of my ingenuity and quick thinking. But then I heard a wet cough and the baby's face twisted into a cartoon expression of displeasure.

And then it started to cry.

The only real experience I have had with babies was watching them on television. And what I discovered that day is that a baby crying is nothing like what you see on TV. First, the baby's face screwed up in an expression of shocked outrage. Then, the mouth opened far wider than any mouth reasonably should. And then this noise came out that was like a hand reaching into my gut and twisting.

I tried everything I could think of to get the baby to stop. I clapped him on the back in case any milk went down the wrong pipe. I sang the first song that came into my head: Jimmy Buffett's "Margaritaville." I made silly faces and barnyard noises to accompany the silly faces. But the baby just kept crying.

Liz walked outside, her arms crossed around her chest. "What's going on?"

"I gave it some milk and I think it might have choked on it."

Liz glanced down at the capsized mug with milk dribbling into the dirt. She smiled and shook her head. "Infants can't drink from mugs. They need bottles. Or nipples."

"Yeah, well, I'm kind of new at this, so excuse me if I don't know the proper infant etiquette," I said.

Instead of storming back into the townhouse, which is what I deserved at that point, she laughed, her head bent over and her hands now holding her stomach. And then I started to laugh, looking at the weird infant and the mug of partially spilled milk and the fact that I was sitting Indian-style in the dirt making cow noises. And then, miraculously, the baby stopped crying. It looked at Liz, then at me, and, I swear to god I'm not making this up, it started to coo.

"Well look at that," I said.

"So how did it get here, anyway?" Liz asked, her arms returning to their original position around her chest.

"No clue. But it wasn't me."

"I know," Liz sighed. "It's just been a stressful day, and the last thing I needed was some weird," she gestured vaguely in the air with her hands, "I don't even know what."

"A lot of essays to grade?"

"Sure. And a lot of students who just can't cut it this semester." She looked over at a blue jay that had just alighted onto the fence. "The community college has this message that anyone can get a higher education. But sometimes," she said, her eyes fast on the blue jay and its ostentatious blue feathers, "that just isn't true."

Whenever Liz made statements like this, usually at the end of the semester after many long meetings with difficult students who threw tantrums when she failed them, a secret compartment within me opened to reveal a coarse, ugly question: Is this what Liz actually thought of me? Did she secretly group me in with the rest of the losers who couldn't handle a basic English course at a community college? I had never tried, of course, having no concrete notion of what I would even want to study, but the question remained: did she think I would succeed, or had she weighed my academic potential in the scales behind her eyes and found me lacking?

"Any more full-time positions open up?" I asked.

Her eyes flashed and grew hard, like a membrane flicking solidly into place before plummeting into the blue-black water. "Sometimes I think it would be nice to get out of here. Just toss all the furniture onto the sidewalk and move out west. Maybe Arizona. Doesn't that sound nice?"

"You want to move out to Arizona?"

She shrugged and said "Just kidding," in a voice that implied that she wasn't.

"So what are we going to do about that?" We both turned to the infant, who was currently paddling his little fists through the air as though he was swimming across a vast ocean.

I assumed the best reassuring yet authoritative voice that I could muster, the words resonating in my throat in a deep, low bass. "I can handle whatever this thing throws at us."

Liz raised an eyebrow. "If you say so."

The next morning I woke up at 6am despite the fact that I didn't have to work. It was still dark outside, though the sky was just beginning to lighten, the window limned in a soft blue. Beside me I could see the small rise and fall of Liz's shoulders, her breathing barely a whisper. She was sleeping in an oversized t-shirt, the kind she only wore around the house with her hair pulled back by a bandana. Usually when she went out, she wore a teacher outfit, a jacket or blazer over a pair of black pants, and then, by a few precise substitutions, it became a poet outfit, a shawl replacing the jacket or a long, flowing skirt replacing the pants. Each outfit was fastidiously put together and contained no less than three or four separate pieces. But

I preferred her careless outfits, the ones thoughtlessly thrown together that allowed her beauty to radiate quietly from her without effort or guile. And I especially liked that I was the only one allowed to see her this way; everyone else had to settle for the made-up version of Liz buffeted by specific images she had of herself: teacher, poet, woman.

And she was all of these things, no question. She used words like "disquiet" and "sonorous." She read small books on the craft of poetry and said that the prose was "knocking her down and lifting her right back up." She sent off poem after poem to literary journals and received small, weightless envelopes of rejections. She had two or three poems published on small, online journals, but she wanted more, and the gradual accumulation of those impersonal rejections was starting to pull her mouth down into unhappy lines.

Once downstairs, I peeked at the submerged baby through the sliding glass door. It appeared to be asleep, its head tucked towards its chest like a bird. Not knowing what else to do, I settled on the floor with Blue curled up against my side to watch some television. The channels flicked by until I came upon a rerun of *Deadliest Catch*.

One winter when we were still dating, I had driven thirty minutes through treacherously icy roads during a freak snowstorm to visit Liz in her apartment. She had read obscure poem after obscure poem to me and I had tried desperately to enjoy the pretty but incomprehensible words twisted together like twine. In return, I had introduced her to the Allman Brothers and Creedence Clearwater Revival and the Beatles' *White Album*. I could tell that this was a relationship that had potential when she updated her Facebook status to include "Bad Moon Rising" as one of her new favorite songs. Although I had always preferred "Fortunate Son," I wasn't about to haggle over the details. One particularly cold night while the trees outside silently trembled their burden of snow, we watched a marathon of *Deadliest Catch*, Liz snuggled in the crook of my arm. In a quiet voice, she asked if we could go out on my uncle's boat next summer, and I had felt a tingly sort of excitement at the thought that this soft yellow hair might still be nestled in the crook of my arm several years from now.

Liz's alarm went off at eight, and her shoulders drooped with disappointment that the baby had not magically disappeared in the night. After she left, I tried to return to the television, but I could see the baby just start to move out of the corner of my eye. He lifted his head, stretched his tiny, delicate arms, and then glanced towards the sliding glass door. I had the urge to feed him some milk, but the cup debacle yesterday was still fresh in my mind.

There was an easy solution though: I could go buy a bottle and some formula.

I knew how Liz would react. She would tell me how ridiculous it was to spend money we didn't have on this visitor. Whatever this thing was in our backyard, it wasn't our job to take care of it. Who knows—it might not even need food.

But still, I felt this aching pit in my chest whenever I thought about the baby sitting in the ground under the blazing sun, hot and hungry and miserable, with nobody to care for him or feed him. I hopped into the car, a decision already reached.

Pulling into the parking lot of the Babies R' Us, I felt an overwhelming sense of unbelonging. Everywhere was the color purple: the sign, the corral for parking carts, the mysterious barrel-like structures at the front of the store.

Inside, I was greeted by row upon row of baby items: toys, wipes, and enough clothing to cover every kid in Salisbury. The few other customers in the store were mostly plus-sized women pushing oversized shopping carts. The few men in the store trailed silently and obediently after the women, listening to their litanies of complaints and needs. A middle-aged woman with a large, toothy smile and a purple nametag made a beeline for me, her hands clasped together in front of her. She was obviously there to weed out the creepy predators and had spotted me, the man with the dirty t-shirt and furrowed brow who clearly didn't belong. In another second, she would sweep me out of the store with as little fuss as possible so as not to alarm the actual families.

"Yes, sir, is there anything I can help you with?"

"Uh, yes," I said, "Where are the bottles?"

She led me through the first row of baby items to an entire shelf of bottles, pacifiers, and other assorted items.

"And what is the name of your little bundle of joy?" she asked, her grin never disappearing from her face. I stared at the woman's mouth and eyes crease-lined from too much sun or smoking or both. As I searched for an answer, the woman's grin began to falter. I was taking entirely too long to think of my own child's name.

"Jack," I finally said, a name I had always liked and the first to pop into my head.

Her grin reappeared in all its former glory. "What a lovely name! And where might the Misses be? Leaving you here to fend for yourself?"

"She's teaching today." I replied much more quickly since it was, technically, the truth.

"Oh, how lovely. My little ones love their teachers, especially Mrs. Johnson who teaches third grade English over at Parkside. That isn't your wife, is it, by chance?" Her face was maniacally hopeful.

"I'm afraid not. Her name is Elizabeth Schultz."

"I see. Well, I'm sure she's just lovely as well. You let me know if you need anything else, Mr. Schultz."

My heart lurched at this name plastered over my own. I wanted to correct her, to blurt out the name of O'Neal and have her say, oh yes, sorry, Mr. and Mrs. O'Neal, but I had not yet broached the topic of whether or not Liz would take my last name, should we get married, and I found that having this perfect stranger mistakenly call Liz, Mrs. O'Neal was worse than being called Mr. Schultz.

At that moment, I wanted to get out of the store as quickly as possible. I grabbed a set of bottles in soft, pastel colors and some formula. The pacifiers were right next to the bottles, and it made sense to get a pacifier in case the baby started crying again. And then, as I was passing by an enigmatic sign that advertised Boppies (whatever they were), I saw a rattle in the shape of a giraffe and I just couldn't resist. After swiping my credit card quickly so I wouldn't notice the total, I tucked the bag against my chest like a football and ferried my purchases out into the sudden blaze of the parking lot, the sun overhead like a wide, unblinking eye.

When I walked into the house with my purchases, I could hear Blue whining and turning in circles. A few steps into the living room, and I could discern why: the baby was crying again, seemingly without end. I dropped the bags and tore into the backyard. His face was screwed into the most miserable expression and a sound like apocalypse was coming from his mouth.

I ran inside, and following the directions as closely as I could, I heated the formula, tested it on my wrist like I had seen on TV, and then, when it was warm but not too hot, filled the bottle with it.

Gently, I placed the bottle up to the baby's lips, and miraculously, it grabbed hold of the rubber nipple and began sucking. By the time it was done, almost all of the bottle was gone.

I sat down on the ground beside the infant, feeling capable and strong. Then, remembering what else I had seen on TV, I patted the baby's back until it belched: a tiny sound like love.

Several days passed like this. I would secretly buy more formula, give it to the baby, wash the bottle and then hide it, all before Liz got home. I wasn't sure how long I could keep up the charade, but it seemed likely that the situation would eventually resolve itself, and I couldn't help but feel proud at how good at all of this I was. At night, I would reach my hands through the covers to grasp Liz's thigh, trail my fingers to the wet, warm cuff between her legs, and every third night or so, she would acquiesce and turn her head to face me. Lately she had stopped initiating on her own, but she continued to receive my advances with genuine warmth, so I wasn't too worried. That night, I climbed on top of her and thrust into her with slow, deep movements. She clutched at my back and moaned softly, and without even realizing it, I strained to hear the sounds in the background, the perpetual drip of the showerhead, the sound of our black lab shifting position, and the soft ticking of the bedside clock, all the while listening for the sound of a baby crying.

On Wednesday, I decided the time had finally come to broach the subject of finances with Liz. I walked into the living room where she was sprawled on the couch watching some reality TV show.

"We need to talk," I said as gently as I could. She remained glued to the TV, as if she was intensely interested in whether or not the designers could, in fact, make it work.

"We've been spending a lot of money lately," I said, feeling less and less assured as I went on, "and the long and the short of it is that we need to cut back."

There was another long silence while an extremely effeminate man discussed the merits of the color fuchsia. I wanted to reach into the television and wring his tiny little neck. And then Liz faced me, her expression tight and controlled. "Do we? I find that fascinating. I really do."

Sensing a trap, I decided to stay quiet.

Liz hopped off the couch and walked through the kitchen to the sink. She looked down at the drying rack, where I had left two bottles and a rattle.

"Ah, yes," I said, feeling the guilt of a puppy whose owner was pointing at the pee-stained carpet.

"So we're in dire financial straits and you're going out to buy toys?"

"Those aren't toys." I realized that the rattle was, in fact, a toy.

"Listen, I've been thinking this over." Her voice had the timbre of finality to it, as though she had already made a decision. "The neighbors have been giving me dirty looks and one of them issued a formal complaint to the office."

Outside, the baby was cooing and waving its tiny fists into the air. I could hardly believe that anyone could have a problem once they laid eyes on him.

"If we don't do something soon, we're going to get evicted."

"All right." I tried to keep my voice calm. "What did you have in mind?"

"We need to get rid of it."

My mouth gaped open. "What are you talking about? We can't just get rid of him."

"It's not ours."

"I know."

"This is not our baby."

"I *know*."

"Who knows if it even is a baby?"

"He's alive, at least."

"It's not our responsibility."

"He…I think it's a he."

"If we don't move *it*, we're going to get evicted," Liz emphasized.

"All right, fine. What do you want me to do about it?"

"Pull it out," Liz said.

"What, like, out of the ground?" I stared at the tiny baby, his face one of complete trust.

"Yes, out of the ground," Liz snapped. "We can't have this noisy thing outside anymore. Pull it out."

I couldn't explain to her my reticence to comply; after all, this wasn't our baby or anybody's baby. This was just a thing sticking out of the ground that happened to look remarkably like an infant. I could tell we were at a pivotal point in our relationship; if I refused, stuck to my guns, protected this little baby at the expense of her feelings, she would storm back into the apartment and mentally begin scanning the real estate listings, forever closing a mental door against my entreaties and apologies. We wouldn't break up today or even a week or a month from today, but we would begin a slow decline into steeled expressions, squared shoulders, and icy non-conversations. So I walked outside, placed my hands on either side of the baby, and tugged.

At first nothing happened. The baby was stuck pretty firmly in the ground, as though he had grown roots. Liz's voice became shrill as she repeated her command, "Pull it out!"

"I'm trying," I screamed back, my voice much higher than I would have liked.

After several seconds of tugging, I heard a snap and the baby came flying out of the ground, dirt cascading from its body. When I looked down to see the baby's legs and feet, they were so consumed by dirt they were almost black. And then, looking closer, I noticed that they were small and twisted and shriveled, exactly like roots.

The baby looked at me for a moment, its face registering utter shock as it hung suspended in the air. Then it let out the most terrible shriek I had ever heard. It was one of those gut-wrenching howls of interminable pain pulled from the very center of the infant's core, the place nobody could touch. It was the kind of noise that made you realize, deep in the center of your being, that everything is terribly, desperately, wrong.

Liz plugged her ears and stared at the baby in horror. "Make it stop!"

Maybe it was that piercing noise of desperation without hope of reprieve. Maybe it was the way Liz was looking at me with those wide, accusatory eyes, as though I was somehow responsible for this mess. Maybe it was that twisted, ugly tangle of root-legs that filled me with a kind of dread. All I know is that I snapped.

"You make it stop," I said and tossed the baby at her.

I saw the baby sail into the air, hands still working furiously at nothing. I saw the baby hit Liz's stomach and I saw Liz instinctively back up, like she was getting hit with a soccer ball. And then I saw the baby drop to the ground and stay there.

All at once, the crying stopped.

If we were in a hospital, this is what would be known as asystole (in the common vernacular we no longer use: a flat line). The bumps and curves that signal the electric impulses from the heart are gone, leaving tiny elevations in the line as the heart struggles to live and fails, which creates the long, held note of the machine synonymous with death.

For a couple of moments that felt like days, we stared at the too-still baby with the tangle of root-legs lying still at our feet. And then, slowly, barely perceptibly, it began to shrink. At first, the movement seemed like the flutter of its hands, but as we watched, the baby grew smaller and denser, its wrinkles compressing into a space the size and consistency of a peach pit. And then, the roots began to wrap around it until all that was left was a small, black nub.

Liz and I bent to peer closer, both of us trying to work up the courage to touch it or suggest that the other touch it. We both straightened and looked at each other, trying to figure out what to do next, how to keep ourselves from going insane as we tried to process this last mind-boggling piece of visual stimulus.

"I'm going to go do the dishes." Liz walked through the sliding glass door, leaving me alone with the not-quite-baby.

As I stared at the small, black pit, I tried to reason through the last couple of days. Certainly, this couldn't have been an infant. Infants don't have roots, and if they die, they don't shrink into blackened prunes. But regardless of logic's firm, cold suggestions, I couldn't just leave the prune baby lying there or surrender it to the police. So, after grabbing the only shovel-like instrument I could find (a large serving spoon from the kitchen), I dug a tiny, shallow grave. Once he was buried, I grabbed a stick lying a few feet away and jammed it in the ground to serve as a marker. When I stood up, the whole thing looked ridiculous and sad—a tiny stick marking an equally tiny patch of upturned earth next to a rhododendron that threatened to consume them both. A mourning dove sang its repetitive song of lament beyond the dying sun. I tried to think of something to say, to remember or memorialize this not-quite-infant who wasn't even mine, but for the life of me, I couldn't form any coherent words. Then I turned and walked into the kitchen to help Liz with the dishes.

A couple days later, Liz and I were lounging on opposite ends of the sofa, watching an episode of *Deadliest Catch*. We were both wrapped up in our own thoughts when we heard the mail slot creak open and a letter drop through onto the floor. Liz and I glanced at each other; it was 5pm and the mail had already arrived several hours ago.

Liz got up and walked to the door. When she returned, she was holding a small, square envelope. It had both of our names in a loopy cursive with no address, no stamp, and no return address. It must have been hand delivered, possibly by one of our neighbors. Inside she discovered a card. On the front was a cartoon stork posed mid-flight with a small gray bundle hanging from its beak.

Inside, the typed font read: Congratulations on your little bundle of joy. Underneath the message was another message in the same loopy font of the envelope. It read: A baby is a blessing and a miracle. Congratulations. All the same, could you try to keep the noise down?

It took a moment for the message to register. We both seemed to understand simultaneously. Liz set the card on the kitchen table, the same cartoon stork looking up at us in mockery. Then, she started to laugh. Not knowing what else to do, I laughed too. We both laughed for a solid minute, listening to the sounds of our sanity slowly unraveling. Then we went back to the sofa and sank down onto the well-worn cushions that belched up their stale old dust and crumbs, the detritus of our lives together.

LOST

Josephine, or Jo as she likes to be called, has a terrible sense of direction. She gets lost going to the bank, the post office, the grocery store, even the 7-11 on the corner with her favorite orange slushies. All of the roads look the same to her; landmarks are meaningless piles of wood or concrete. She turns right when she should turn left, goes straight when she should turn around, and often feels the sickening knife-plunge of certainty when she hits the outskirts of town and realizes she's been heading in the wrong direction. It sometimes feels as though the world is being erased behind her—each rut in the road removed as soon as she bumps over it, only to reappear in her mind when she loops back around.

She has developed elaborate tricks for finding her way home, such as drawing a decreasing series of numbers on stop signs, light poles, and small dogs tethered to tree trunks, creating a trail of breadcrumbs she will recognize. Her friends often make fun of her:

Poor Jo couldn't find her way out of a paper bag!

Poor Jo—if she ever gets married, she'll have to handcuff herself to the man so she doesn't forget and wander off.

They laugh their high-pitched laugh that reminds Jo of sharpened teeth and tell her they are only joking.

One day she runs into the little sign wishing she would come back soon and thinks, why not keep going? People travel every day. Maybe she can find a place she will remember, a place that will imprint a map in her mind. So she keeps driving.

After a few minutes she realizes she can't remember her home very clearly. She pictures the knobby plaid couch and the bowl of beaded fruit on the kitchen table, and then, as she drives further away, the sweep of blue curtains in the window, and then nothing at all. She takes this as a sign that she is headed in the right direction.

She stops at sprawling rest stops in Georgia and discovers dozens of different pecan products. She continues through the Carolinas and Virginia, stopping briefly around the Eastern Shore of Maryland. She wants to see crabs, but instead she finds geese, herons. She stops at a low-slung brick restaurant serving Steaks Seafood Pasta. When the waitress tells her they don't serve crab, a man in the adjacent booth gives her directions to an all-you-can-eat crab buffet that she knows she will never find. Already the twists and turns accompanied by the easy sweep of his hands are disappearing from her mind. She thanks the man and eats her Fettuccine Alfredo.

She reaches the endless mountains of Pennsylvania with town names like Tunkhannock, Towanda, Wyalusing. She finds a dingy motel on Rt. 6 where a gum-snapping waitress serves her a huge slice of pie for a dollar fifty. There are red farmhouses, gleaming silos, the occasional cluster of goats. Several times she must stop for roadwork, a large woman in a bright yellow vest flicking her wrist to find another route. Since she has no clear destination, Jo doesn't panic as she is forced down thin, looping side roads, the pavement falling away in chunks near the edge.

She continues to the fog-smeared towns of Maine and finds a whale-watching cruise. Next to several tourists in red and blue windbreakers with children clutching digital cameras far too expensive for their stubby fingers, Jo watches two whales swim right up to the side of the boat. For a moment, she is thankful for the obliteration of her memory. She waits for them to break the surface and arc a beautiful spout of water, but they never do. Underneath the water, pale and ghostly, they glow.

Jo means to continue up into Canada to try some maple syrup, but instead she drives south and west. In the fields of Belvue, Kansas, her car breaks down. It was only a matter of time before a gear slipped in all the miles she was driving. She walks down a small dirt road and sees a man idling on a lawn mower. She asks him where the nearest hotel is. Her hair is disheveled and her eyes rimmed with black. The man holds the soft white flesh of her wrist and forces her to stop. He leads her to a tan farmhouse and places her between soft blue sheets.

When Jo wakes up, she notices gauze-like curtains ruffling against an open window. Sitting up further, she touches the cream-colored comforter, the light blue sheets beneath them. The sheets are not as soft as she remembered: they are starched stiff and both ends are tucked underneath the mattress. She wiggles out of them carefully. Glancing around the small room, she sees a book-case, a braided rug across the hardwood floor, and a small, frosted light above her bed.

There is a knock on the door, and then the same man enters with a tray. Jo has never seen a man whose face was quite so square. There are the beginning of fine wrinkles near his eyes, and his hair is cropped close to his head. He is the kind of man others would call stocky, but Jo prefers sturdy. She's never really cared for men who bend like willows. She prefers men more solidly anchored to the ground.

"Thought you might like some breakfast." He places the tray across her lap. "You seemed awfully tired."

"Thanks. What's your name?"

"Benjamin." He wipes his hands on his jeans and reaches out to shake hers.

Jo waits for Ben to ask her name, but he doesn't. He just stands there and watches her eat. When she finishes, he takes the tray and closes the door gently behind him. On a small chair beside the bed, there are a towel and a washcloth. Jo opens and closes doors until she finds a bathroom with black and white tiles. She takes a long, hot shower. Hanging on the back of the door are a pair of jeans and a sleeveless blouse. The blouse is only slightly loose on her, but the jeans fit perfectly. She wonders what other needs this strange man has anticipated. She knows she should be wary of him, of a serial killer basement hidden beneath the floorboards, but Benjamin's every move has the air of a large man trying not to crush something delicate.

Downstairs, she finds Ben washing dishes. When he sees her, he turns off the faucet and leans back against the sink.

"Hope the clothes fit alright. They were my sister's."

Jo notices the past tense, but the information feels much too intimate to pursue.

"I had your car towed to Bert's auto. Hope you don't mind. Turns out your timing belt snapped. I can take you up there this afternoon."

"Thanks." Jo rubs the silky material of the blouse between her fingers. "Why are you doing all this?"

Ben shrugs. "Just feel like it, I guess." There is a brief silence and Ben clears his throat. "So, do you know someone here?"

"No," she says, "Just travelling."

"Where are you headed?"

Jo shrugs, feeling suddenly shy. There is no way she can explain why she has been drifting from town to town, unmoored. If she tries to explain how objects lose their permanence as soon as she turns her back, he would just roll his eyes and tell her to learn how to read a goddamn map or explain, as though talking to a child, how nobody's memory could be that bad. She just needs some mnemonic tricks like Please Excuse My Dear Aunt Sally. That was how every other person from her mailman to the 7-11 clerk had responded when she first tried to explain her bizarre affliction. She's come to realize that most people have an unshakeable view of the world, and she doesn't fit within it. So now she just keeps it to herself.

"Well, if you don't have any particular place in mind, why don't you stay here and rest a bit longer? No one's using the guest room, so you're free to stay a couple more days."

"Okay," Jo says. Resting for a couple more days does sound nice. The road will still be there, after all.

Over the next couple of days, Jo learns more about Ben. He drives an hour and a half each day to the Hostess factory where he supervises the line. Jo can imagine the donuts—chocolate and powdered and glazed—all ferried down belts to be packaged in gleaming white bags. It's mostly all done by machine now, he explains, so there isn't much to the job. She asks why he doesn't live closer to work, and he explains how the farmhouse used to belong to his parents. When his father died of heart disease and his mother succumbed to early onset dementia, he and his sister meant to put it up for sale. The second day of her visit, as she was driving to the real estate office, she was killed by a garbage truck that ran a red light. Now, the house is all Ben has. Everything else has been shucked from his life.

When he asks about her parents, Jo clamps her mouth shut. She can only remember pieces of her childhood, brief images unattached to anything else: a wooden mailbox with their last name etched onto the side, a plastic box filled with buttons of all shapes and colors. She can't remember the house at all, and whenever she asks her mother, the description seems to change slightly each time. Both of her parents moved out west to Arizona, shedding furniture and decorations in their wake in an effort to live a smaller, more simplified life. Jo is embarrassed to admit that she can't even remember whether her mother has brown hair or blonde hair until she looks at the photograph of all three of them taken at the Smile Hut when she was fifteen. (It is probably gray now, anyway.) She keeps the photo in her wallet for reference so they don't disappear completely.

Each night Ben makes dinner, roasted chicken or pasta with meat sauce, and tells her stories from his life. He always leaves a small silence at the end of each in case she wants to tell one of her own. At the end of the second week, instead of walking into the guest room Jo is starting to think of as hers, she opens the door to Ben's bedroom. Quietly she climbs into the king-sized bed. The sheets are just as stiff as in the guest bedroom. She tells him about her life, what she can remember up until that point. She tells him about travelling all across the country and how she could never return to the places she's been, including her home, because she can no longer remember the way. Afterwards, he is quiet for a while.

"Well?" she asks. "It's ridiculous, right? Unbelievable?"

"We all have something," he says and traces an invisible line down her thigh.

For a couple weeks, everything Jo needs—toiletries, books, the ingredients to chicken divan—Ben brings back for her. The day after she slept with him, she was preparing a trip to the mall to buy some clothing, but Ben had grabbed her wrist, just like when she had broken down in front of his house, and asked her to stay. His eyes were large and they trailed down to his sister's gingham shirt. "Whatever you need," he said, "I can get for you." Sometimes Jo imagines that when he saw this woman in his sister's blouse and jeans standing there, suddenly and irrevocably whole, it was an image he could never let go.

And for a while it was okay. She read the well-creased paperbacks from the used bookstore and occasionally made casseroles from whatever ingredients Ben brought home. But now, her memory is getting worse. Earlier that day she walked into the front yard, looked up at the white-hot smear of sky, and felt the pitch and stagger-step of panic before she turned and remembered the house, how to get back inside. At the same time, she can hear her feet tapping the rhythm of the road: the steady ca-chunk, ca-chunk of the highway that hasn't been paved in years, the rat-tat-tat-tat when she drifts into grooves lined into the median. She thinks about all the places she hasn't seen and is surprised to find the aching yawn of desire bloom inside of her. It is only a matter of time before she walks out the front door and drives through the fields of Kansas and out of Benjamin's life forever.

Later that night, Jo finds Benjamin stirring a pot of chili for dinner.

"I can't stay locked up here."

Ben continues to stir without looking at her. "And a map won't help?"

Jo shrugs. "The streets don't mean anything to me. They don't tell me what I'm trying to find."

He pulls out a sheet of paper and spreads it across the kitchen table. The edges hang off the side, and Jo wonders where it came from. He pulls out pencils, pens, markers, a compass and ruler. With aching precision, he begins drawing a map. She can see lines and circles begin to take shape: first, his house, and then the street leading down to the corner mart. She can see the post office, two grocery stores, the Super Wal-Mart, and their neighbors' houses. More of the same, she thinks to herself.

He asks her about the house where she grew up, where she had her first dance, her first kiss. She can't remember and she waves her hands in the air, stirring the fog of her memories. His questions get more specific. Where was a place you made a promise you later broke? When was the first time you knew your mother would eventually die? Answering each question solidifies her memories, pulls them into light. She describes the taste of her mother's chicken divan, the nutcracker suite from her grandfather kept on the mantle year-round. He pulls out interstate maps, guides to every state. He runs his finger down passages on places of interest and asks her follow-up questions. He finds even more obscure books that zoom in to counties and streets, that pan through the ever-shifting landscape of mailboxes, that hover over backyard barbecues where tree branches have been stripped into swords, a series of captured moments that were once true. Every so often he thrusts a book at her with his finger jabbing a photo and she cries yes, that was my friend Sallie's house or that was the hospital where I was born.

With each nod he draws more lines, the map growing larger and so finely detailed until it is a tapestry with a million silky threads, a tree trunk carved with the rings of her life. When she looks at it, she can see their house and through the tiny window, the packet of seeds on the dresser he meant to plant later that day.

He creases the paper into an intricate series of folds. Only a small square is now visible.

"Just refold the map to show where you are." He hands her the hard lump of paper, heavy from such accumulation.

"Test it out," he says. "We need some stamps from the post office."

She traces her finger down the street from their house until she finds the right building. It is all so simple. She gets in the car and drives slowly, pausing every few moments to check and recheck the map. Cars honk at her in intersections, but she ignores them. Finally, she makes it to the post office. Once she is back in her car, the route back wavers like lines of heat off asphalt. She studies the map, finds Benjamin's house—our house, she thinks— and the way back crystallizes. She can clearly picture the yellow farmhouse with the meadowsweet planted out front. Ben, too, she can remember: the curly brown hair on his back and chest that reminds her of seaweed, the way he holds his hands like two meaty paddles he hasn't yet learned how to use. She sticks the map on the dashboard and glances at it every now and again to make sure she is headed in the right direction. When she makes it back home, Benjamin is visible through the window. He smiles and waves, and her breath feels heavy and warm inside her.

Days pass like this. The map is fine, amazing really, but having to work her way through the intricate system of folds to find the one area she needs is tiresome. One day she leaves the map in the car and feels a small knot of guilt at how much lighter she feels. Can she say for certain she will never lose the map, either leaving it on the counter while paying for gas or letting it tip out the car window? She needs something quicker, lighter, more permanent. She looks down at the fine creases on her palms that a fortune teller would use to link the past and the future, and she has an idea.

In the living room, she pulls out the markers Ben used to create his map. She draws a map on her body, starting with the very tips of her fingers. There are lines like capillaries leading to all of the places she has been. She winds a pink path down her stomach, circles the small hump of her thigh. She has symbols for all of the important places. A circle for her childhood home. A triangle for the hospital where she was born. A heart on her wrist for Benjamin.

After she finishes, she walks outside and drives to the grocery store. She feels a tenuous system of roots winding their way around her, each line leading her back. She buys eggplant and bread crumbs and sauce, a watermelon for dessert. All the while she thinks about what jobs she will apply for, what she actually wants to do with her life. As she loads the bags into her trunk, it begins to rain. No, she thinks, but it is too late—the lines blur and slide down her body. She hadn't used permanent ink. The heart too smears into an angry red lump and she can no longer remember what it is supposed to mean. She panics, opens the trunk, looks at the groceries she just purchased. They are strange, meaningless. Who needs an entire watermelon for one person?

She closes the trunk, gets into the car, and drives, feeling an itch at the small of her back that she can't quite reach. It blooms, a soft beckoning of nail, until she doesn't notice it any more.

HUNGER

Through the window that overlooks the backyard filled with honeysuckle and buttercups, Mary can see two children, a boy and a girl, emerge from the forest at the edge of her property and stand blinking in the sudden light. The girl wears a pink dress with tattered white ruffles and the boy, a pair of overalls somewhere between blue and gray. Both children are filthy— leaves sticking out of their tangled hair, their faces mashed with dirt, as though they have been wandering the forest for days. Mary sets down the dishrag she had been using to dry her lunch dishes and walks outside.

She clears her throat until the children see her and stop. They are frozen in place like a game of Red Light, Green Light. "I'm sorry, but are you lost? Do you need help?"

The boy looks at the girl and then slowly nods his head. His fine yellow hair is slicked with sweat. He reminds Mary of the little boys whose mothers have smothered their hair in gel for Sunday service.

Mary waves them inside and they walk in, silent. The girl sucks her tiny white fingers. They can't be more than seven, eight years old.

Mary runs a bath in her chipped porcelain tub and washes their clothing in the downstairs sink. When they emerge, their hair dripping on her nice hardwood floors, Mary forces a smile and says, "There now, that's better."

Though she is forty-five, Mary has no children of her own. Her husband died ten years ago in a car crash on his way home from the pharmacy. (The police were able to recover the stapled white bag filled with his blood pressure medicine, which Mary kept on her dresser for two weeks, unable to throw it out). When she finally folded herself around that splintering grief, she found she had no desire for children any longer, no desire for their piercingly small fingers, their incomprehensible secret language, their shedding of mittens and shoes and socks when you weren't looking.

The girl places her fingers back into her mouth. Well, Mary thinks, at least now they are clean. She turns to the boy who seems to be older, if only by a year. He has a slight harelip and his tongue darts nervously across it.

"What are your names?" Nothing.

"Who are your parents?" Nothing.

"Where do you live?" This time the boy points out the window toward the forest.

"Yes," Mary says, trying to hold her irritation in check, "but where? What street?"

The boy says nothing and she decides it is useless to ask for a phone number. Perhaps they are still exhausted and shaken from their journey through the woods. She's walked that forest a few times and it is always much larger than she imagines. As soon as she has passed between the thick oak trees, the light is swallowed by a canopy of leaves and the brush seems alive with quick-footed creatures. In the shadow of the leaves she can sometimes see the gleam of wet fur.

"Are you hungry?" Both children nod frantically. At last, she thinks, now we are getting somewhere.

She walks into the kitchen and boils a pot of water. She doesn't have a lot of food—she found her appetite diminished with her husband's death. When he was alive, she would make pork chops and casseroles and whole roasted turkeys along with a heavy mound of buttered vegetables, the smell drawing him from his study. He would eat each meal slowly, bite by bite, his gratitude escaping in small sighs. But now, she will eat maybe half a turkey sandwich for lunch, a couple bites of chicken breast for dinner. She pours the entire box of spaghetti into the roiling pot. There will be leftovers, but these children look hungry, and it is better to have too much.

When she brings in the platter of spaghetti heaped with sauce and covered in a layer of grated parmesan cheese, the children's eyes are sharp and green. The room is quickly filled with the meaty sound of their chewing. They eat the portions she has served and then reach for the tongs. After ten minutes, all of the spaghetti is gone. Two sets of eyes turn to her, and inside them the path is endless.

"We're still hungry," the boy says.

At least they're talking, Mary thinks. Not wanting to lose this morsel of communication, she offers to make chocolate chip cookies, and this is met by more furious nods.

After she has mixed the dough and set the timer and pulled the warped cookie sheet from the oven, the children pluck the cookies from the heated metal before it has even cooled, leaving brown smears like mud across their cheeks. They look up at her again. It hardly seems possible they are still hungry. She brings out an entire block of mozzarella cheese, two plastic containers of smoked turkey, and a loaf of wheat bread for sandwiches. The boy twists open the plastic wrapper and eats one slice of brown bread at a time while the girl shoves chunks of cheese into her mouth.

Mary walks into the kitchen and opens her pantry. What could curb their voracious appetites? She has a few dented cans shoved in the back: green beans, kidney beans, sweet potatoes and creamed corn, and these she opens and places on the table, not even bothering to spoon it onto a plate. The children suck down the mush and drain the liquid too. She brings out jars of mustard, mayonnaise, and relish and the children lick each glass clean.

She walks back to the kitchen for more, but her pantries are empty. The children have eaten everything she has. When she returns to the table to tell them that she is sorry, she catches them devouring the plates, white shards of porcelain glinting from their lips.

"No! Stop that!" Mary gathers the shards in her palm. "Those aren't for you."

The boy and girl look up at her with eyes wide like little brown mice. They wipe the dust from their mouths. Mary carries the shards to the kitchen and lays them on the countertop. The biggest piece still has a bright orange cluster of milkweed. She had chosen the pattern as a wedding present because it reminded her of the fields of Pennsylvania where she and her husband had grown up, hiding behind drenched bales of hay after a sudden summer rain.

Back in the dining room, she can hear a sound of splintering, cracking. She finds the children breaking the legs off of the table and shoving the ends in their deep red mouths.

"Please," she says but the children continue chewing, the wood creaking under the strain of their tiny white teeth. Their fingers are dirty and full of splinters. They finish the table and move on to the chairs, and from there, to the pictures of her and her husband hanging on the wall.

Mary watches as they devour her wedding photos, starting with Aunt Kathy and Uncle Edward with his sodden-looking toupee, moving on to her husband's brother (the one in and out of the hospital all last year with cancer of the liver), and finally arriving at the beaded train of her wedding dress, her husband's cowlick and his thin, guarded smile. He never liked being the center of attention, preferring instead the quiet solitude of one of his dusty hardbacks. On their first date, she had had to draw him out with pointed questions, like "When is the last time you ate an entire cake by yourself?" and "Where is your favorite place to listen to the rain?"

And then, suddenly, all of those people are gone and it is as if they never existed in the first place.

At that point, the boy and girl split up, perhaps to cover more ground. The boy climbs the stairs to her room, and she can hear the squeak of the bedsprings and then a very loud crash, most likely the dresser. The girl begins stripping the frame of the window and slurping down strips of wallpaper like spaghetti. She unwinds the braided coil of the rugs, rips pages from her husband's books, Hemingway and Faulkner and Joyce, and shoves them rolled into her mouth. She even curls her lips around light bulbs. Mary winces when she hears the glass shatter.

Finally, the boy returns and helps the girl rip the door off of its hinges, the burnished doorknob her husband bought at an antique store falling uselessly to the ground. When they begin pulling up the floorboards, Mary runs outside, her head in her hands. She cannot bear to watch any longer.

It takes them several hours to peel away the layers of wood and insulation and wiring until they reach the dark gray mortar of the foundation. This they scrape into their hands and sprinkle over the few remaining items: a couple of baseboards, a cracked window pane, and a blue and white cushion heavy with stuffing. When they finish, they sit in the now-empty lot full of tamped-down dirt, licking their fingers.

"Thank you," they say, "that was good."

Mary marches up to them, pointing a finger in their dirt-smudged faces. "Get out of here. You've left me with nothing. Go home."

The children stand, their eyes now a muted shade of hazel, and disappear through the trees. Mary sits in the dirt and listens to the frenzied cry of a Carolina wren—

teakettle, teakettle, teakettle. With nothing else to do, she traces a finger in the dirt until it becomes the outline of her husband: the glint of his round glasses, the solid heft of his shoulders and neck. Her breath blossoms inside her. She places him in their house, using her nail to detail the gauzy white curtains, the frayed ends of their rugs. Once filled, the house looks more solid somehow, like it could bear the weight of both of them. She can hear her husband rooting in the fridge for something to eat. For a moment, the birds are silent. She opens the door and walks inside.

ACKNOWLEDGMENTS

The following stories have appeared in the following journals:

"Roadkill" — *Prick of the Spindle*
"Barley" — *The Speculative Edge*
"My Father Is an Angry Storm Cloud" — *decomP*
"Girl Band" — *Petrichor Machine*
"Protest" — *34th Parallel*
"A Haunting" — *Northwind*
"Grade A" — *Columbia College Literary Review*
"Baby Blues" — *Flywheel Magazine*
"Lost" — *The Quotable*
"Hunger" — *Paper Nautilus*

ABOUT THE AUTHOR

MELISSA REDDISH is the author of a flash fiction collection, *The Distance Between Us* (Red Bird Chapbooks, 2013). Her stories, poems, and reviews have appeared in print and online journals. When not writing, she teaches English and directs the Honors Program at Wor-Wic Community College. She lives on the Eastern Shore of Maryland with her husband, dog, and cat, where she does stereotypical Eastern Shore things like eat crabs smothered in Old Bay and go for long walks down by the water with her black lab. She blogs very occasionally at melissareddish.com.